"So...date me."

Wait...what?

"We'll tell people we met when you came for your interview, and that we instantly connected and got to know each other online. And once you moved here, we took it to the next level."

The next level?

"I mean a relationship—like dating," she said quickly. "Not *that* level."

"I've already figured out that conversations with you are an adventure, but you lost me on this one. I have no idea what you're talking about."

"You and me, pretending we're a couple until everybody gets to know you."

Callan blinked. "That's not a thing people really do, Molly. In movies, maybe, but not in real life."

"Somebody must have done it or they wouldn't have known it was a thing that could be a movie plot."

Would every conversation with this woman be this utterly ridiculous? "We've never been attacked by aliens or survived a zombie apocalypse, but they've managed to make quite a few movies about them."

"We've never been attacked by aliens that you *know* of," she corrected. Then she shook her head sharply, as if to wipe the thoughts out of her head. "Anyway, back to us being a fake couple so you're not single anymore."

"We could never pull that off."

She grinned. "Of course we could."

Dear Reader,

Sometimes while you're writing a series, a secondary character will take hold of your heart and you know the muse won't rest until that person finds their true love. In the case of my Sutton's Place series, that character was Molly Cyrs, friend of the Sutton sisters. As soon as Molly stepped onto the page, I knew I was going to give her a happily-ever-after and *Falling for His Fake Girlfriend* is her story.

Callan Avery has come to Stonefield, New Hampshire, to be the new librarian, and the last thing he expects is to find himself pretending to date the woman next door. He's a man who likes order and Molly is a bit of a chaos gremlin, but to save his job, they'll convince the Stonefield community they're falling for each other. They don't expect it to actually happen!

You can find out what I'm up to and keep up with book news on my website, www.shannonstacey.com, where you'll find the latest information as well as a link to sign up for my newsletter. You'll also find links to where I can be found on social media, where I love to connect with readers.

Welcome back to Sutton's Place, and I hope you enjoy Callan and Molly's story!

Shannon

Falling for His Fake Girlfriend

———

SHANNON STACEY

Recycling programs
for this product may
not exist in your area.

ISBN-13: 978-1-335-72439-7

Falling for His Fake Girlfriend

Copyright © 2022 by Shannon Stacey

For questions and comments about the quality of this book, please contact us at CustomerService@Harlequin.com.

Harlequin Enterprises ULC
22 Adelaide St. West, 41st Floor
Toronto, Ontario M5H 4E3, Canada
www.Harlequin.com

Printed in U.S.A.

A *New York Times* and *USA TODAY* bestselling author of over forty romances, **Shannon Stacey** grew up in a military family and lived in many places before landing in a small New Hampshire town where she has resided with her husband and two sons for over twenty years. Her favorite activities are reading and writing with her dogs at her side. She also loves coffee, Boston sports and watching too much TV. You can learn more about her books at www.shannonstacey.com.

Books by Shannon Stacey

Harlequin Special Edition

Sutton's Place

Her Hometown Man
An Unexpected Cowboy
Expecting Her Ex's Baby

Blackberry Bay

More than Neighbors
Their Christmas Baby Contract
The Home They Built

Carina Press

Boston Fire

Heat Exchange
Controlled Burn
Fully Ignited
Hot Response
Under Control
Flare Up

Visit the Author Profile page
at Harlequin.com for more titles.

For my boys. Sometimes I forgot your field trip permission slips or you were almost late to school because the clean clothes were still in the dryer, but you navigated having a chaos gremlin for a mom with humor and grace. Now you're men and I'm so proud of you both, and grateful for you every day.

Chapter One

After decades of serving our community, today is Carla Denning's last official day as Stonefield's librarian, so stop by and wish her a very happy retirement! If you miss her, she'll be staying unofficially for a few more days to help our new librarian settle in. Mr. Callan Avery becomes the keeper of the card catalog tomorrow, and we wish him the best of luck!
—Stonefield Gazette *Facebook Page*

One of Molly Cyrs's favorite things to do was sit at the small window table in the Perkin' Up Café with her journal open next to a rich, *very* caffeinated beverage, and watch people. Whether they were customers inside or pedestrians on the other side of the glass, it amused her to watch her fellow residents of Stonefield, New Hampshire—many of whom she'd known for her entire life—go about their business.

This morning, she was trying very hard not to stare at the hot guy who'd walked through the door a moment ago. She was failing pretty miserably, but at least she hadn't been caught watching him.

Yet.

The man was tall, but not *too* tall. Molly liked guys who could reach the top shelves at the store, but who weren't so tall they'd always be looming over her. And this one was big without being bulky or too muscular. Not a dad bod, exactly, but he had nicely rounded edges and a great butt. Men who were super into their bodies weren't Molly's type. She'd dated one once, and the first time he'd gotten judgmental about her having a Little Debbie snack cake, she'd kicked him to the curb.

This man had hair almost as dark a brown as hers, and his skin was creamy pale under a neatly trimmed beard. They were all a little pale in Stonefield right now, even though it was the end of April. It had been a long, frigid winter and a cold rainy spring, so they all needed some sun.

Black-rimmed glasses were perched on his nose, and she wondered if he really needed them to see, or if they just completed the image that the black slacks and pale blue button-up shirt made. He looked like a businessman who'd forgotten his briefcase. Businessmen weren't really Molly's thing, either—too many schedules and phone alerts—but he was nice to look at.

After he'd been handed his coffee order and glanced her way, he held her gaze for a long moment and she got a better look at him. And when he started toward her, she got to see that he had dark brown eyes behind those glasses.

"You're Molly Cyrs, right?"

Did she know this man from somewhere? She didn't think so. She would have remembered him, business type or not.

"Callan Avery." He didn't wait for her to respond before he put out his hand.

The feel of his skin against hers distracted her for a moment. It wasn't exactly soft, but he had no calluses and his nails were very well groomed. A second too late to keep it from being awkward, she remembered herself and dropped his hand. "Why does that name sound familiar to me?"

"I'm the new librarian."

"Oh, right. That's why." So his look was *librarian*, not businessman. As far as Molly was concerned, the librarian vibe was one-hundred-percent more sexy.

"Thank you. I know Mrs. Denning held the position for a long time, so I have some big shoes to fill."

"I'm sure you'll do great." She refrained from adding that a *lot* of people weren't sad to see Mrs.

Denning retire. She could be cranky and she should have retired a long time ago.

The search for a new town librarian after Carla Denning announced she was retiring had been very thorough and, though she wasn't privy to all of the details, Molly knew her father—who was on the board of selectmen—had been very satisfied when they offered the position to Callan Avery because he was the best man for the job. To Paul Cyrs, that meant not only was the man qualified, but Paul thought he'd better the community in some way. And her mother was on the library committee and had been directly involved in hiring him, so she obviously thought so, too.

"I'm also your new neighbor," he continued.

"That's right!" She smiled brightly at the reminder. She hadn't seen the buyer of Mrs. Bright's little house next to her family's home, but she'd heard from Daphne Fisk—the only and therefore the best real estate agent in Stonefield—that the new librarian had bought it. "Welcome to Stonefield, neighbor."

"Thank you. I have a question, though, and it's a little…odd."

"Have a seat," she said, gesturing to the empty chair across from her. "You've come to the right place for odd."

When his eyebrow arched, she replayed her words her head and winced. That hadn't come out exactly right, but she knew from experience that if she tried to explain, she'd only make it worse. He was sitting down, so she hadn't scared him off, and her curiosity about his question was stronger than her desire to explain she wasn't *odd*. Mallory Sutton, her best friend, called her quirky, which she much preferred. But mostly she had ADHD and an unsinkable positive attitude, so she could be a lot for people who weren't used to her.

"I have some concerns about living next door to a funeral home," he said, his gaze locking with hers as he turned his cardboard coffee cup around and around in his hands.

Good Lord, his eyes were dark. Molly was sure they must be brown, but they were so dark a brown, she could barely discern his pupils. Darker than chocolate, even. His eyes were the color of black coffee, she decided, and though she preferred her coffee with lots of cream, it definitely worked as an eye color.

"Molly?"

"Oh, right." Her cheeks heated because losing track of time was the usual for her, but losing track of time because she was staring so deeply into a man's eyes was new. "The funeral home. Well, it's been there well over a hundred years, so it wasn't a surprise."

The brows over those delicious eyes dipped. "What do you mean?"

"You knew the funeral home was there when you bought Mrs. Bright's house."

"Of course I did."

Molly was growing more confused by the second. "If you knew it was there, what's the problem?"

He was frowning now, shaking his head. "I didn't say there was a problem. I said I have an odd question."

Of course he had. Molly took a sip of her latte and then smiled, determined not to derail the conversation again. "What's your odd question?"

He considered for a long moment, and then sighed. "There's really no delicate way to phrase this. How will I know when there's going to be a funeral?"

"Well, somebody will die."

The low growling sound of frustration he made was one she was very familiar with. Her father made it often, her teachers had practically worn out their vocal cords doing it, and sometimes random strangers she had to deal with made it. "Molly, I'm being serious."

"So am I," she replied. "If somebody dies, you'll know there's likely going to be a funeral at Cyrs Funeral Home because we're the only one in town, and if nobody dies, we probably won't be having a funeral because that's…not how it works."

"I am aware of how funerals work," he said in a terse voice, and Molly sighed.

It was a shame he didn't appear to have a sense of

humor. It was very difficult to date in a town with such a limited pool of available men—men she knew too much about, seeing as how she'd grown up with most of them—and it was even more difficult when the funeral home was factored in. Even though she only helped her mother in the office, handled what little marketing they did, and assisted loved ones during viewings and funerals, her job made prospective boyfriends uneasy. She had almost no luck bringing men home with her, even when she explained she had her own apartment over the long garage where the hearse and two dark sedans were parked.

For the most physically attractive man she'd seen in years to not only have a personality that would clash horribly with hers, but a possible aversion to the family business was just mean.

And disappointment had a way of coming out in her voice as annoyance. "We don't have a neon *open* sign, if that's what you mean."

"That's not at all what I mean." After a few seconds, the corner of his mouth tilted up in what was almost a smile. "I'm sorry. I get tense when I'm uncomfortable with a conversation."

"Fair warning, then. You're probably going to be pretty tense around me a lot. I'm great at talking, but not so great at conversations."

"I don't understand."

"My impulse to talk works faster than my brain can process what's been said and figure out what I *should* say next." She gave a little shrug. "I usually think of the right thing to say hours later. Usually at two in the morning when I'm trying to sleep."

His body relaxed and amusement warmed his eyes. "Tell you what. If you *don't* knock on my door at two in the morning to respond to something I said hours ago, I'll keep in mind conversations with you will be an adventure and try not to be tense."

She wouldn't mind having future conversations with him. There was something about the way he looked at her that made her want to squirm in her seat, and she wondered if he looked at everybody that way. Surely not. "It's a deal."

"Good. So I'll start over," he said in a *much* more relaxed tone. "I'm remodeling the house, and I don't want to have power tools running or the music too loud or anything while a funeral is going on. I want to be a respectful neighbor, but I'm not sure how I can plan for that other than reading the obituaries every morning, and that's not how I like to start my day."

"Oh." And here she was thinking he was being a jerk when all he was trying to do was be kind. "That's really considerate of you."

"If there was a way for me to find out in advance when you'll be having a service, that would be helpful."

This was her opening. She barely managed to get a hold of her facial expression before a triumphant grin took over, but she cleared her throat and tried to sound serious. It wasn't her natural state of being, so it took some effort. "You and I can exchange cell phone numbers and I'll text you when we'll be hosting a viewing or a funeral."

"That would be wonderful, thank you." He recited his number and after punching it into her phone, she sent him a text with her name—bonus, he'd have the correct spelling, which wasn't *Sears*, just in case he hadn't noted it on the elegant sign at the house—and watched him save it to his contacts.

She thought he'd get up then, but he gave her a curious look. "Since I already asked one odd question, I guess I'll add another out of sheer curiosity. Do you write the obituaries?"

"No, my mom helps the family craft them." She sighed. "She tried to hand that off to me once because it's time-consuming and she's busy with other aspects of the planning, but I guess my creative flair for drama and writing obituaries aren't a good match. They're not really meant to be entertaining."

He obviously didn't know what to say to that—and honestly, what *could* he say—but she got another smile out of him. A genuine one this time, with his teeth showing and his eyes crinkling at the corners. And his gaze lingered on her face, dipping to her mouth before returning to her eyes. She suddenly felt too warm in her sweater and she could feel the rush of heat showing on her cheeks.

"I should run," he said abruptly, standing. "It was nice to meet you, Molly, and thanks for your number. I'd say I look forward to hearing from you, but that would be weird."

She laughed, making heads turn in their direction. "It was nice to meet you, too, Callan."

When he walked away, a quick glance around the café told her everybody had gone back to what they were doing, so she was safe to watch him walk. Not only did he have a really great butt, but he obviously liked books and did have a sense of humor, after all.

Maybe he was more her type than she'd initially thought.

Callan wasn't sure he'd ever met a woman as confusing as Molly Cyrs, but he thought about her during his entire walk back to the new house he was determined to turn into a home.

She was beautiful, with long dark hair pulled into a ponytail, and dark eyes that sparkled with humor. Even though she'd been sitting, he could tell she was tall and slim, and she'd been wearing a sweater with a mermaid on it. If asked an hour ago, he would have said a grown woman wearing a mermaid sweater was ridiculous, but somehow it suited her. It was colorful and fun, and she seemed as if she had a fun sense of humor. And she was definitely cute.

As he turned the corner onto the street, his gaze caught on the sign for Cyrs Funeral Home, which was a massive Queen Anne–style house that dominated the corner. Like most funeral homes, the property was immaculately kept, with gardens and a lot of parking. It was on a lot equivalent to at least four of the usual residential lots in the area.

Then he reached the tall white stockade fence that separated the Cyrs property from his. It was obviously meant to offer some privacy for mourners. And also for him, because large numbers of people tended to mill around outside funeral home events when the weather was nice.

And then he was past the nice white fence and his not-as-nice white house came into view. The clapboards needed paint—or vinyl siding—and the dark green shutters had faded and chipped. Considering the condition of the house, he'd been surprised by how well the yard and small flower beds had been kept, but at least that was one thing he could cross off his renovation to-do list. And maybe it was a small thing, but he'd take anything he could get.

When he'd been informed the position at the library was his, he'd reached out to the local real estate agent for help in finding a place to live. Daphne had found several places for rent, but they were all small apartments downtown, above businesses or in old homes that had been converted into apartment buildings. Callan was tired of apartment living. He wanted to put down roots, so after several thorough video tours and a lengthy email Q&A, he'd bought this house sight unseen. He had no regrets, but he'd definitely taken a dive straight into the deep end and was in over his head.

Right now the house was nothing more than a mostly empty and very outdated box. And it was a small box, too—just a tiny Cape with two small bedrooms upstairs, made even smaller by the slanted ceilings due to the roofline. The only bathroom was at the top of the stairs, and it was barely big enough for the toilet, vanity and the tub-and-shower combo he'd bleached until he almost passed out from the fumes.

Downstairs, there was a kitchen and dining area combined, a living room, and a family room he was using as a bedroom for now. While he'd have to navigate the stairs many times a day because there wasn't even a half bath downstairs, he didn't want to hit his head on the ceiling when he got out of bed every morning.

Buying a house with one bathroom and appliances as old as him hadn't been ideal, but it had a garage and he could walk to work. The only other property he'd considered had two and a half bathrooms and had been remodeled in the current century, but it was a huge Colonial that would have cost half his salary to heat and he would have had to drive to work every day.

So he'd make do, and slowly fix it up. Maybe by the time he was done, he'd be ready to flip it and move on to something bigger. Something with a proper library, maybe. For the foreseeable future, his car would have to stay outside in the driveway because the movers would be arriving in a couple of days with so many boxes of books, he would have to put them in the garage.

Today's mission was a drive into the city. Stonefield had a decent-size market and he'd been told the local thrift shop had an excellent collection of almost anything he could need. But for a major stocking up, it was worth the time and gas to have a bigger selection and lower prices. He'd been adding things to the shopping list on his phone since he arrived in town, and he winced as he scrolled through it, doing a final check.

Five hours and an obscene amount of money later, he sank onto the pastel floral couch Mrs. Bright had left behind, too tired to even wince anymore.

But he had a fairly well-stocked kitchen now, and new linens to add to what he'd packed in his car. Cleaning supplies. And, of course, the biggest television he could fit in the car with everything else. It wasn't very big, but he didn't watch a lot of TV. It would do for now.

After a short nap on the world's oldest and least comfortable couch, Callan forced himself to make some dinner. It had crossed his mind to walk to the diner because he wasn't going to meet people by staying in, but he didn't have the energy tonight.

Maybe tomorrow, he thought as he sautéed some chicken to go with the potato "baking" in the microwave. It was the one appliance that could be considered updated, and he was thankful for it. The dishwasher, on the other hand, was a lost cause, so he washed the few dirty dishes he'd made by hand and looked at the magnetic whiteboard hiding at least some of the lovely gold freezer door. There was so much to do, as far as unpacking and starting to remodel, that he had to write a few priorities on the whiteboard to keep himself from bouncing from task to task without finishing any of them.

He was debating on where he wanted to start—graphing out a new kitchen layout or unpacking the box of random living room things—when his phone rang. It was his FaceTime ringtone, so he knew before he fished the phone out of his pocket that it was Roman McLaughlin. He was the only person on the planet Callan would do video chatting with, outside of work meetings at his previous library.

Rome was a good friend—probably the best Callan ever had. He was the kind of friend who helped you move apartments three times in two years, and when you owned as many books as Callan did, that was a big ask.

"Hey, Rome," he said after he'd hit the button to bring his friend into view. And the view was the same as it was 95 percent of the time—Rome's office. He was in finance, and the very definition of workaholic.

"Hey, Cal. You look good. I was expecting you to be more pixelated and glitchy."

Callan snorted. "I'm in New Hampshire, not the Alaskan bush."

"If you can buy bear spray at the local gas station, I'm just going to assume the cell signal will be sketchy."

Callan laughed, but he couldn't deny the cell signal and internet options were among the first things he'd researched about Stonefield when considering applying for the library job.

"So what's going on?" he asked, because he knew he had five minutes at the most. Rome wasn't a call-and-spend-some-time-catching-up kind of guy. He touched base with frequent short calls that invariably ended with a quick *I've gotta get this, so I'll call you back* and a disconnection beep.

"Have you met anybody yet?" Rome asked.

Callan rolled his eyes because he knew Rome didn't mean *anybody*. He wanted to know if Callan had met any possible future dates yet, and it was startling when an image of Molly from the café flashed through his mind. She was *not* a possible future date, no matter how pretty she was, because they'd barely been able to get through one conversation without it falling apart in several bizarre and confusing ways.

Maybe if he'd been relaxed when he met her instead of all nerved up about approaching a stranger about an awkward topic, they would have started off on stronger footing.

"I've only been here a few days," he pointed out.

"It took you a minute to answer that, so you *have* met somebody."

If Rome didn't love video chats, Callan could have lied and said he got distracted by putting milk away or something. But since Rome could see him, all he could do was hope he didn't blush. "I haven't met anybody I'm interested in dating, Rome."

That was the truth, at least. He'd met an incredibly sexy woman whose laugh turned him inside out, and who popped into his head at random moments. But he wasn't going to date her. Maybe he'd chosen Stonefield because it was the kind of place he'd like to raise the family he was ready for, but he wasn't going to rush into anything.

"We're not getting any younger," his friend said. "And I'm pretty sure when you buy a house in a small town, getting yourself a wife is the next thing by default."

"Who are *you* dating, Rome?"

Silence.

"Yeah, I didn't think so. If your office had a shower and a closet, you would never leave it."

"Plenty of time, Cal."

"Oh, so plenty of time for you, but not for me? We're the same age, my friend."

"Yeah, but you drink all that coffee. I'm going to live longer than you."

Callan laughed, but the mention of coffee made him think about Molly again. He hadn't dated in a while because he'd been busy, and then he didn't see the point when he knew he'd be leaving NYC, but that still didn't explain why he couldn't stop thinking about that woman.

"Did you call just to give me a hard time?"

"No, I called to wish you luck on your first day at the new job tomorrow. I mean, also to see if you landed in a town full of attractive, single women who find books incredibly sexy, but mostly to wish you luck."

"Thanks. I'm looking forward to being out of an admin office and back behind a circulation desk again."

"I don't understand the appeal of leaving the office and having to talk to people but— Damn, I've gotta take this. I'll call you back."

Callan smiled when Rome's face disappeared, and he slid the phone back in his pocket. He had maybe a 20 percent success rate with getting a goodbye in before calls with his friend ended, but he didn't mind. He liked it, even, because long conversations drained him and he found them difficult to extricate himself from. That was never a problem with Rome.

He would have liked a chance to argue the benefit of leaving the admin office behind, though. Being behind a circulation desk was different. There were a lot of conversations, but they were usually short, and centered around things Callan loved to talk about—books and information, and how to find it.

Tomorrow was going to be a very good day.

Chapter Two

Congratulations to Sutton's Seconds for being voted Best Thrift Store in New Hampshire for the second year in a row! Those of us who live in Stonefield aren't surprised because Ellen Sutton has been providing us with quality used goods for many years, but it's wonderful to see her hard work recognized!
—Stonefield Gazette *Facebook Page*

One of the first things Molly did every morning, after sitting in the overstuffed reading chair and setting her coffee mug on the side table, was open her notebook. The chair was next to the window to let the sun wash over her, and this bright tableau was how she liked to start her days.

The notebook was a simple running to-do list, with a few notes and ideas scattered among the tasks. It really had no organizational structure, but that worked for her. She'd tried other systems, from basic to complex, but her brain just liked to write down things she needed to do and then draw a line through each thing as she did it. Each morning, she'd flip through the pages and copy three things onto a sticky note from the small basket next to her coffee mug, and those three things would be her focus for the day.

1. Order a replacement for the colonial blue vase that was chipped during the Harrington viewing.
2. Make an appointment for an oil change.
3.

Molly realized she'd been looking at the blank number three without turning any of the pages of her notebook for a while and sighed. Then she took another sip of her coffee, hoping it would jump-start her focus. It didn't, and she knew why.

3. Have hot, sweaty sex with the new librarian.

She didn't actually write the words on the sticky note. Only tasks that were directly in her control got transferred over because she could only control herself, and making sure she accomplished the three priority tasks for the day was how she managed to wrangle her ADHD brain into getting things done. If she wrote *Dad needs to see the optometrist* on her sticky note, it wasn't in her power to accomplish that. But *catch Dad in the office and make him call the optometrist in front of me* could be checked off.

Having hot, sweaty sex with the new librarian wasn't a task she alone could accomplish. It would require active participation from Callan Avery, and she doubted he'd be on board. Sure, she'd seen some flashes of heated interest in his eyes, but she'd also seen facial expressions similar to his from several ex-boyfriends, and she knew what they meant.

You're just too much for me, Molly. You're a lot.

She *was* a lot. She was also worth it, though she hadn't found a man who agreed with that yet. But she would. Someday.

After flipping through the pages of her notebook one more time, she decided to leave the third spot blank. There was nothing starred to denote urgency, except for getting the oil changed in her car, so two tasks would do.

Or maybe she needed more coffee. Espresso would be nice, with a big jolt of caffeine to get her through the morning. Nobody made a macchiato like Chelsea Grey—literally, because nobody else in Stonefield made anything but plain coffee with a hot or iced option—so Molly got dressed in a cute sweater over soft leggings. Then she took the time for some mascara and lip gloss before grabbing her notebook and heading for the door.

She walked, as usual, but at a quicker pace than she normally did because she knew what time the library opened and if she was going to "accidentally" bump into Callan, she had to hurry.

As soon as she stepped through the door of the Perkin' Up Café, Molly scanned the room, but she didn't see him. Doing her best to hide her disappointment, she stepped up to the counter to order her macchiato since she couldn't really change her mind and leave at this point.

"I didn't expect to see you here today," Chelsea said.

"I'm here all the time."

"But rarely on a Wednesday, and almost never two days in a row." Chelsea gave her a knowing grin. "And you don't usually look around the room so intently, like you're trying to find somebody."

"I'm nosy."

"Or *waiting* for somebody. That looked like an interesting conversation you had with the new librarian yesterday. Some smiling, some frowning, and I'm pretty sure I saw you blush at one point."

Molly took her macchiato and, after rolling her eyes, carried her beverage and her notebook to her regular table. Because it was everybody's favorite table, due to the window, it wasn't always open, but today was clearly her lucky day. After taking her first sip, she closed her eyes and savored the highly caffeinated deliciousness while thanking the coffee gods yet again that Chelsea Grey was a part of her life now.

Chelsea Grey had moved to town and opened the Perkin' Up Café two years ago, and since then, she'd become a good friend. Molly liked having a friend who hadn't grown up there and didn't already know every single thing she'd ever done in her life.

Mallory Sutton had always been—and would always be—her best friend, though. She was the middle Sutton sister, and Molly was also close with Gwen, who was the oldest, and Evie. Molly was an only child and growing up, she'd practically been a fourth Sutton sister. And David and Ellen Sutton had been like a second set of parents.

David's had been the hardest funeral the Cyrs family had ever hosted.

Gwen and Evie had both been living elsewhere when their father passed away. When they found out months later that their father had mortgaged everything to pursue his dream of opening a brewery and taproom, they'd come home to help their mother and Lane Thompson—Evie's ex-husband and David's business partner, which had been pretty awkward when Evie found out—because if they didn't open it, Ellen would lose everything.

Now Sutton's Place Brewery & Tavern was a thriving business, and Gwen and Evie had fallen in love and stayed. All three Sutton sisters married and living in Stonefield made Molly so happy, she grinned every time she thought about them. And she thought about them a lot.

She took an Instagram photo of her drink and then took a very small sip. Taking up a table once your drink was gone struck Molly as rude, so she was always careful to take her time drinking whatever she ordered if she wanted to linger.

Finally, the bell over the door chimed and Callan Avery walked through the door.

His hair was still slightly damp from a shower and Molly sighed. She knew he probably smelled delicious and wished she could think of an excuse to go to the counter, where she could stand close enough to inhale his scent.

But that would be creepy—as she was reminded every time some guy did that to her—so she kept her butt in her chair and watched him from the short distance instead. Maybe she stared so hard he could sense it, because as soon as Chelsea stepped away to make his coffee, Callan turned to face Molly.

She smiled and gave him a little wave, and he returned the smile before turning back to the counter. Molly didn't mind. Having his back to her gave her the freedom to appreciate the way his pants hugged his butt, which had enough curve to make her hands itch to slide over it. A white business shirt was tucked into the pants, but he'd skipped the tie. That was probably a good move in Stonefield. He didn't want people thinking he was stuffy.

When Chelsea handed Callan his coffee, Molly assumed he'd leave since it was almost time for the library to open, but he turned and walked toward her.

"Good morning, Molly."

"Good morning. What do you get?" she asked, nodding at the cup in his hand.

"Coffee."

He said it so matter-of-factly, she wasn't sure if he was trying to be funny. "Just plain coffee, huh?"

"Yeah. She makes some damn fine coffee. What's yours?"

"Macchiato today, because I was in the mood for one. But usually I don't decide in advance. I come and then order what I'm in the mood for in the moment."

"In the moment, huh? That doesn't surprise me."

She wasn't sure if that was meant to be an insult. She didn't think so, but she was so used to her impulsiveness being criticized, she bristled a little. "Have you ever tried a macchiato or have you been drinking your plain old coffee the same way since your very first cup?"

"When I like something, I don't feel a need to change it."

"Then you miss the opportunity to maybe find something you'd like even more."

He shrugged. "I guess that's a risk I'm willing to take. So do you come here every morning?"

"Not *every* morning, no. I usually treat myself two or three days a week, but I had that craving for the macchiato this morning." She'd actually had a craving to see *him* again, but she wasn't about to confess that. "Do you want to sit down?"

When he shook his head, she wasn't surprised since she knew what time it was. "Thanks, but I have to hurry if I don't want to be late on my first day."

"Another time, then," she said, dropping as obvious a hint as she could without actually asking him out.

"Maybe. I'll see you later." Then, without giving any indication he'd gotten the subtle message, he turned and started walking away.

"Have a good first day at work," she called, expecting him to pause or lift a hand to show he'd heard her.

But he stopped and turned, giving her a smile that took her breath away and made butterflies dance in her stomach. "Thank you, Molly."

And then he was gone, leaving her sitting there feeling like a cartoon version of herself, with heart eyes and a cloud of sparkles shimmering around her. That man had quite a smile.

Callan's first day as the head—and only—librarian at the Stonefield Library was a disaster.

His plan had been to have a great first day, then walk home and spend some time stripping his new living room of old, stained wallpaper.

Instead, he was going to walk home, take some acetaminophen and try not to beat his head against said ugly wallpaper.

Carla Denning, who was retiring after spending her entire adult life as Stonefield's librarian, wasn't quite ready to leave. She'd suggested staying on for several extra days to introduce him to the collection, their patrons and the way things were done. Callan had wanted to roll up his sleeves and get to work, because the way things were done was so outdated it was like going back in time.

He'd only been given a brief tour during his interview, but it had been enough for him to see that the discolored and tattered cards in the old wooden card catalog needed replacing—either with new cards or a computer system. He could see with a cursory glance at a few shelves that it had been so long since the collection was weeded, it wouldn't surprise him to find an original copy of *The Catcher in the Rye* shoved between a Betty Crocker cookbook from the fifties and a manual for how to use rotary phones.

But he didn't want to insult Mrs. Denning, so he kept his mouth shut, his hands off the dust, and just listened. Unfortunately, on several occasions, he also had to listen to the departing librarian explain to patrons that, yes, relatively young and single men could be librarians. He knew over 80 percent of librarians identified as female, and he could only guess none of the other 20 percent had ever worked in *this* library.

Then he heard her telling a parent on the phone that, no, their daughters didn't need a chaperone because they'd done very thorough background checks on Mr. Avery and he was very nice and very safe, even though he didn't have a wife. That was a half hour before a man asked Mrs. Denning for a list of the library committee members so he could complain about the hiring because he didn't want some guy hitting on his wife when she went into borrow some more of those romance books.

If he hadn't sold everything he had of value and gone into debt to buy a house, Callan might have quit on the spot. He'd been warned that small New England towns could be tough nuts to crack, but this was ridiculous. He also wanted to point out that having a wife and children didn't preclude him from hitting on married women or being a predator, but he didn't think that would help his case any.

"It'll be fine," Mrs. Denning told him, giving him a patronizing pat on the hand. "It'll take a little time for them to get used to you is all."

It had been a frustrating day overall, and during his walk home, he turned the issues over and over in his head. The only solution he could come up with—Mrs. Denning's advice to give it time and let them get used to him—seemed too passive for him. If enough people were uncomfortable with him being alone with the patrons, which was something so out there he hadn't even considered the possibility, and complained to the library committee, they could rescind the job. The contract he'd signed had a thirty-day probationary period built in, but he'd been assured it was boilerplate and he had nothing to worry about.

Maybe they'd been wrong. And maybe he should have rented an apartment after all, and settled into the community before buying a house. Hindsight and all that.

He was frowning, caught up in the ramifications of being fired his first week, when he turned the corner to his street and almost walked into Molly Cyrs. She made a startled sound, her hand flying up to cover her chest.

"Excuse me," he said, reaching out a hand to steady her. "I wasn't really paying attention to where I was going."

"Me either," she said with a smile. "Fair warning, I'm rarely paying attention."

"I'll keep that in mind." Despite her prediction he'd often be tense around her, the opposite happened. When she smiled at him, some of the stress from the day slipped away. "That's not the first time you've said 'fair warning' before telling me something about yourself, you know."

"I come with a lot of warning labels, but enough

about me. How was your first day?" she asked brightly, and then her smile faded. "It doesn't *look* like you had a very good day."

Callan's frowned deepened, his expression at odds with the realization he needed to do a better job of schooling his face so nobody would know he was already frustrated at the library. "It was interesting."

"I heard some stuff."

Of course she had. "There was so much stuff, I'm almost afraid to ask which stuff you heard about."

"There were a lot of people who didn't expect the new librarian to be a sexy single guy."

His face betrayed him again, this time with a flush of heat across his cheeks. "I didn't hear the word *sexy* used."

"I did." She gave him a cheeky grin. "Several times."

"I'm more worried about the parents who think their daughters need chaperones to be in the library with me."

Concern replaced the amusement in her eyes. "Oh, that's not fair to you. I'm sorry."

"No, it's not fair, but I'm a stranger. Mrs. Denning thinks once people get to know me, it'll be fine."

She tilted her head, her eyes scanning his face. "But you don't think so?"

"I think I can win people over. But there are complaints going to the library committee and I'm just afraid they're going to let me go before I get the chance." He shrugged one shoulder, shooting for a casualness he didn't feel. "I guess if I was older, or I was a family man, it wouldn't be a problem."

"Or less sexy," she added. After looking him up and down, she sighed and shook her head. "I don't think you can do anything about that, though."

He wasn't sure how he felt about the word *sexy* being used to describe him around town, but he liked the fact Molly thought he was. "Should I stop washing my hair or trimming my beard? Maybe add some spaghetti sauce stains to my shirts and burp in public?"

She considered the questions as though they'd been sincere, but he could see the mischief dancing in her eyes. "No, you'd probably still be sexy, but then we'd have to be mad at ourselves and question our taste in men."

"Well, since you claim I can't un-sexy myself, and I can't make myself older or married overnight, I guess I'll just have to keep smiling, doing my job and hoping for the best."

"You sound like a man who needs a trip to the taproom. And it's a good night to go because they added being open on Wednesday nights to the schedule a couple of months ago, but they're never really busy."

"The taproom?" He assumed she meant a bar, but with her, he wanted to make sure. It could be a dance studio for all he knew.

"Sutton's Place Brewery & Tavern, which is

owned by my friends. It's super casual, so no pressure. And I work there, so I know everybody. I mean, I don't *work* there, but… I kind of do."

"I don't know what that means."

"I'm not employed by the taproom, but it's fun to be there. And it's owned by my best friend Mallory's husband—and her sister Evie's husband and also their mom, so I can help whenever I want."

Callan was going to need a spreadsheet. "That sounds like a lot of people to meet."

"Trust me," she said, and his skin warmed when she put her hand on his arm to reassure him. "It's going to be fun, and the more you get out, the more people will get to know you and look past that neatly trimmed beard and the lack of spaghetti sauce stains on your shirts."

He thought about his plan to go home and strip wallpaper, but he knew he'd probably just pace the living room, fuming over the situation he'd found himself in today. And he was tired enough so going out and meeting new people sounded daunting, but at least if he was with Molly, he'd probably have a few laughs. And he definitely needed something to lift his mood.

"Okay. I guess I could use a beer after the day I had."

Chapter Three

Stonefield PD responded to a number of complains about neighbors on Juniper Street this week. Several residents are claiming ownership of a cat and each of the reports states the cat loves to roam outdoors but resides at their home. The chief said he'll be following up on veterinary records to ensure the cat isn't being overvaccinated, but as far as ownership, he offers this quote: "I don't believe anybody ever owns a cat. Cats do what they want."

Clearly our police chief has met a few felines in his day.

—Stonefield Gazette *Facebook Page*

Molly loved walking through the door of Sutton's Place Brewery & Tavern. It was almost like a second home to her, probably because it was owned by people who were as much family to her as her own parents.

And she also knew all the customers who turned to look when the door opened. They always did, just to see who was coming in.

She could remember when it was just the carriage house next to the Sutton house, used as a barn for storage, more or less. And she could remember when David Sutton had started talking about brewing beer with Lane Thompson, and then they'd started talking about turning the carriage house into a taproom.

David hadn't lived to see his dream brought to life by his wife and daughters, along with Lane and some help from friends, but Molly could feel him every time she walked through the door. Maybe the warm, friendly spirit of the place would help Callan relax.

Because he'd had a hard day, she grabbed them two seats at the quiet end of the bar. It was a pretty quiet night, and Irish was working it alone. She saw Evie serving some nachos, and she assumed Darby—the young woman they'd hired to work in the kitchen and wash dishes around her classes at the community college—was working tonight.

"He looks like a real cowboy," Callan muttered, and she realized he was talking about Irish, who was never without his battered hat and boots.

"He was. He's part owner now, though, and brews

the beer with Lane. And he's also married to my best friend."

There wasn't time for more explanation because Irish walked over to them. "Hey, Molly. How's things?"

Irish wasn't subtle in the way he looked between her and Callan, but she didn't introduce him. There was a chance the other customers didn't know who he was and that might be for the best tonight. Let him have a beer in peace. "Good, thanks. How's Mallory?"

His fierce look was replaced by a smile. "She's good. She's with the boys in the house, hopefully resting. What'll you have?"

Once Irish had set a beer on a coaster in front of each of them and figured out Molly wasn't going to explain who Callan was or why he was with her, he wandered off to take care of his other customers. But he kept glancing over and she knew he'd be keeping an eye on her.

"This is good," Callan said after taking his first sip. "And this place is nice. I like it."

His approval warmed her, and she hoped being here would give him a little bit of a boost. He'd had a really rough day, and she couldn't imagine what it must feel like to have strangers not welcome you because you didn't fit their perception of who you should be.

It wasn't fair. He'd even gone out of his way to

find out how he could be a respectful neighbor to the funeral home. Since they'd once had a tearjerker of a rendition of "Amazing Grace" during a funeral interrupted by their neighbor on the other side deciding it was a good time to clear his Harley's pipes, Molly appreciated that. And her parents would, too.

"I haven't even made my first mortgage payment yet," Callan said, his voice low. He was staring into the amber liquid in his glass, and for a moment she wondered if it had been a mistake to bring him here after all.

But he'd only had two swallows of it, so it wasn't as if he was drowning his sorrows in alcohol. He was justifiably frustrated, and she really wished she could help.

She didn't think the library committee would fire him for such ridiculous reasons. She knew her mother wouldn't, but it was a small town. The whisper network was efficient and often ruthless, and if enough people got it in their head he should be gone, others on the committee might cave.

And she knew there was a probationary period written into the contract. The committee could simply tell him he wasn't the right fit after all. Callan would have no job and a house he'd just bought in a town he probably wouldn't want to live in anymore.

It was in Molly's nature to help people. She was very empathetic and she also loved puzzling out solutions. She also didn't like when somebody was being punished for something they didn't do.

But there was no way to accelerate being a part of a community. As Mrs. Denning had said, they had to get to know him. That took time. And she knew from a lifetime in this town that negative rumors spread much more pervasively than positive rumors. Just telling everybody he was a great guy wouldn't do any good.

Positive gossip, she mused. A shortcut to being accepted by the Stonefield community. A way in.

She gasped and slapped Callan's arm, almost making him spill his beer. "Come with me."

"What?"

"Just for a minute. Leave your beer." She mouthed to Irish she'd be right back but, judging by his scowl, he wasn't sure he liked her stepping outside with a stranger.

"Molly," Callan said as he slid off the stool. "Where are we going?"

"Just come on. I have something to tell you."

She'd figured it out.

When Callan followed Molly outside, he assumed they were leaving and he worried about the fact they hadn't paid their bill. It was bad enough some of the people in this town thought he'd come to steal their women away. A dine-and-dash wouldn't help his reputation any.

Instead, she walked around to the back corner of the building, where they were out of sight of the entrance and the windows. It was weird, but he was already catching on that Molly Cyrs didn't do things like other people did.

Once she seemed satisfied that they couldn't be seen or heard, she turned to face him. She was practically bouncing on the balls of her feet, and he marveled again at the energy she put out.

"I figured out how to solve your problem," she said, her eyes bright with excitement. She had such expressive eyes, and watching them was making him feel better.

"My problem?"

"Yeah, the whole problem where people were surprised to get a sexy and single guy as their new librarian and you bought a house and it would suck if you lost your job before you even made the first mortgage payment?"

"Oh. That problem."

She rolled her eyes at his droll tone, but it didn't dampen her enthusiasm. "We can fix that."

We? "I don't think there's any way to fix it. You can't buy trust and respect at the market."

"You should date me."

Wait...what? He couldn't have heard her correctly. "Excuse me?"

"We'll tell people we met when you came for your interview, and that we instantly connected and got to know each other online. And once you moved here, we took it to the next level."

The next level?

"I mean a relationship—like dating," she said quickly. "Not *that* level, although people will make assumptions, of course."

"I've already figured out that conversations with you are an adventure, but you lost me on this one. I have no idea what you're talking about."

"You and me, pretending we're a couple until everybody gets to know you."

He blinked. Then he blinked again because in the brief space between blinks, he hadn't come up with anything to say. "That's not a thing people really do, Molly. In movies, maybe, but not in real life."

"Somebody must have done it or they wouldn't have known it was a thing that could be a movie plot."

Would every conversation with this woman be this utterly ridiculous? "We've never been attacked by aliens or survived a zombie apocalypse, but they've managed to make quite a few movies about them."

"We've never been attacked by aliens that you *know* of," she corrected. Then she shook her head sharply, as if to wipe the thoughts out of her head. "Anyway, back to us being a fake couple so you're not single anymore."

"We could never pull that off."

She grinned. "Of course we could."

It would be so easy to lose himself in her sunny personality and be swept away by the force of her positivity. The citizens of Stonefield believing he was in a relationship and on his way to becoming the well-settled family man some of them thought he should be would definitely make his life less stressful. In the short term, anyway. Eventually, he and Molly would have to stage a breakup because they were quite possibly the *least* compatible people on the planet. But, as she'd said, it would give people time to get to know and accept him.

"Who would know the truth?" he asked, despite the fact he couldn't believe he was actually considering this.

"My best friend and her two sisters, because they know I haven't been talking to anybody online, and also because I could never lie to Mallory. And Chelsea, who owns the Perkin' Up Café."

"You think telling the owner of the local coffee shop is the best way to keep a secret?" That would be four people who knew, so the chances it would remain a secret seemed pretty slim to him.

"She won't tell."

"Do you tell each other stuff like that? I mean, maybe she'd believe it."

"Maybe." She shrugged. "Except we were talking about you and she said I should date you and I laughed at her, so she already knows the truth."

"You laughed at her?" He wasn't sure why that

bothered him so much, since he would probably laugh at anybody who'd suggested he date Molly, too, but it hurt a little.

"You're a little too grumpy to be my type."

"I'm not grumpy."

"You've been frowning at me since we met."

It took some effort, but Callan wiped the scowl off his face. "In my defense, the frowning at you has been less about being grumpy and more just being very confused by our conversations. Less grump and more concentration."

She gave a little shrug. "That's fair. But anyway, we went off on another tangent."

"I'm not sure you can call them tangents if we were never headed in a straight direction to start with it. Conversational paths with you are less like jogging paths and more like wandering around in the woods. Which is fine," he added quickly when her smile dimmed. "Wandering in the woods is nice."

"Unless you intended to go for a jog," she pointed out, and then she waved her hand. "Anyway, back to the benefits of everybody thinking you're my boyfriend. First, it means you're a good guy because there's no way I would date you and bring you around my family and the Suttons if you weren't."

"Dating you automatically makes me a good guy?"

"Everybody here knows me, so maybe not *auto-matically*, but it's a bit of a shortcut for you. And as an added bonus, you'd have me to take you out and introduce you to people. I'm very social, so it'll be easier for you to meet everybody."

"What about your parents?"

"Oh, right." She sighed, and then held up her hands. "I think I have to keep them in the dark. They're very involved in the community. He's a selectman and my mom's actually on the library committee, so I think knowing the truth would put them in a tough spot."

"Your mother is on the committee?"

"Yes. Amanda Cyrs? But don't worry, both of my parents were very pro *you*. And I don't usually give them updates on my dating habits, so they won't think it's weird if you and I are suddenly a thing."

He was actually considering it. Not only that, but what she was saying made sense. She was something of an "instant in" with the community he would be making his home. And it would ease the minds of the people concerned about a single man being the only staff member in the library. While he thought that was an ignorant fear and his first instinct was to ignore them, he needed this job to stick and pretending to be in a relationship with Molly seemed a harmless way to smooth things over until they'd all gotten to know him.

"You're thinking about it," she said.

"It makes sense." He snorted. "I don't know how or why, but it does. But what do you get out of it?"

She shrugged. "I get a fake boyfriend and keeping the secret will be a fun challenge. You have to take your entertainment where you can find it in this town."

"Fair enough."

"Also, now I have a plus-one to my friend Gwen's wedding next month."

There was a little voice in his head whispering that this was a very, very bad idea. This was a multimonth pretense she was talking about, and going to a wedding with her—not just as a plus-one, but as her boyfriend—was a big deal. He was getting in over his head.

But that whispering voice was drowned out by the voice shouting that yes, *this* was the perfect solution to all of his problems. Not only would the library's patrons have to get to know him and get over their belief that librarians should be older women with their hair up in buns and reading glasses hanging from chains around their necks, but he'd get to meet a lot of new people quickly. And those meetings would be far less awkward with an extrovert at his side.

"How do we start?" he asked, and the whispering voice sighed in defeat.

"It's easy. First we take a selfie and then, when we go back in, hold my hand. That's all it'll take to get the ball rolling."

Chapter Four

After four decades of taking care of the insur-
ance needs for Stonefield's residents, Barton
Insurance will be closing their doors. The Bar-
tons will be reaching out to current customers
to answer any questions about the transition,
and we wish them a very happy retirement!
—Stonefield Gazette *Facebook Page*

Callan held open the door of Sutton's Place Brewery
& Tavern for the second time tonight but this time,
as soon as he'd stepped inside, Molly slid her hand
into his. He was her fake boyfriend now and everybody in town needed to know it. The boyfriend part,
anyway. She tried not to notice how her entire body

tingled as he laced his fingers through hers, but she *really* liked when he touched her.

That part wasn't fake.

This time when the customers looked to see who was coming through the door, they did double takes. The arched eyebrows and whispers flew, and Molly felt a pang of satisfaction as she held Callan's hand. Her plan was totally going to work.

"Oh good, Mal's here now," she said after spotting her best friend by the end of the bar. "I want you to meet her."

"She's not working, is she?"

Molly laughed. "No, she's not, but even if she was, she can take a couple of minutes to talk. It's not that kind of place and, even if it was, her husband, mother and brother-in-law own the place."

His eyes widened again, and she realized she might have to find the time to make him that spreadsheet after all, or something else to help him keep track. Then he shook his head. "I meant because she looks *very* pregnant."

"Oh, very pregnant. But if she is working, she's not working very hard. Trust me, Irish won't let her overdo it."

Mallory turned her head then, and saw Molly. Her gaze dropped to their linked hands and then back to Molly's face as they approached. "Irish told me you were here, so I came over to say hi but then I thought you left."

"We just went outside for a few minutes so he could take a call. Callan, this is my best friend, Mallory Sutton. Mal, this is Callan Avery."

"Oh, our new librarian," Mallory said, extending her hand. "I've heard a lot about you."

"He's also my boyfriend," Molly added.

Mallory's face froze for several seconds before a forced smile replaced the genuine one. "Okay. I hadn't heard *that* about you."

Callan's smile didn't look much more genuine. "I'm a pretty private person."

"Molly's usually whatever the opposite of that is."

"Exhibitionist?" Molly offered.

Mallory frowned. "Isn't that when you like having sex where other people can see you?"

"I'm definitely not that." Then she remembered she was supposed to be pretending to date the man next to her, and she gave him a smile. "Unless you're into that sort of thing. I guess we can talk about it later."

She was starting to think Callan had literally swallowed his tongue, but then his jaw unclenched and the red faded from his cheeks. "Exhibitionist has a much broader meaning, and this would be the sort of thing two people would discuss privately, so yes, later."

Molly laughed. "I don't have secrets from Mallory."

Her best friend arched her eyebrow, tipping her

head toward Callan. "Except secret boyfriends, apparently."

"It's a long story." Molly shrugged. "I'll tell you later. I want to introduce him to some more people."

Since the point of the ruse was to not only convince library patrons he was taken, but also to shortcut his introduction to the Stonefield community, she stopped at every table. She doubted Callan would remember all the names and faces thrown at him, but they'd remember Molly glowing and holding his hand as she introduced them to her boyfriend, their new librarian.

When they'd spoken to everybody, she started back toward the bar to grab seats, but she spotted Mallory and Evie with their heads close together, clearly talking about her. At least Gwen wasn't here tonight. She was entirely too practical and she probably wouldn't have anything nice to say about Molly's newest escapade. She wasn't surprised when Mallory and Evie walked to where she was standing with Callan.

"We're going to borrow Molly for a few minutes if you don't mind," Mallory told Callan, but judging by the way Evie was tugging on her arm, they didn't actually care if he minded or not.

"Sure," he said, looking anything but sure. "I'll go grab a seat at the bar."

With Evie in front of her and a very pregnant Mallory behind her, as if she'd make a break for it, Molly went up the stairs to the office and storage area.

Evie flipped on the light and then turned to face her. "Since when is the new librarian your boyfriend?"

"Okay, he's really not."

"You just introduced him to me as your boyfriend," Mallory pointed out.

"I did, because we're pretending. He's my fake boyfriend."

Evie laughed for a second, and then she stopped and a frown replaced the amusement. "Wait. You're serious?"

Molly nodded and then, when both women just stared at her, she told them the story as quickly as possible. She didn't like leaving Callan alone when the whole point of them being there was so she could introduce him to people, so she tried not to go off on any conversational tangents. And when she was finished, both women just kept staring at her.

"So that's it," she said, just in case they were waiting for more story.

"I think Gwen would know the right thing to say here," Evie said. "But I don't."

Molly grinned and lied through her teeth. "I think Gwen would be amazed by my brilliant solution to Callan's problem and maybe write it down to use in a book someday."

Mallory snorted. "You're only saying that because

she's not here to tell you that this is probably the most ridiculous thing you've ever done. And I love you, but that was a high bar to start with."

"No, it makes perfect sense," Molly argued. "I can help him get to know everybody and he'll get to prove himself as librarian without all the senseless drama he had to deal with today."

"And what are *you* getting out of the deal?" Mallory asked.

She shrugged. "It'll be fun and I'll have somebody new to hang out with. I love you, but you're super pregnant and Evie has an infant and Gwen's focused on her wedding and, well, just being Gwen."

"Just how far is this pretend dating going?" Evie asked, and Molly knew what she was asking.

"We didn't really define that up front."

"What *did* you define?"

"Only you two and Gwen and Chelsea will know the truth. No parents."

"Molly." Her best friend had a way of saying her name so the single word sounded like a verbal face-palm.

"No parents," Molly insisted. "And no husbands. Or almost husbands."

Mallory frowned. "There's no way Irish will buy this story."

"Neither will Lane," Evie said. "Or Case. You were complaining just last week about the lack of dating material in this town, so there's no way they believe you've had a boyfriend online. Other people might buy that you wanted to keep it a secret until he started his job, but they won't."

Molly frowned because they were probably right. And she didn't want them to have to tell the guys outright lies, or lie to them herself. The more people who knew, though, the higher the chance the secret would stop being a secret. Not only would that be embarrassing for Callan, but the library committee might decide they'd made a big mistake and fire him for an entirely different reason.

"I trust them," she decided. "But *nobody* else, even your mom. She's friends with *my* mom and I don't want her to know because she's on the library committee, so that would put her in a weird position."

"Everything about this is weird," Evie muttered.

"I know, but Callan deserves a fair shot at this job and he's not getting that because some people in this town are being ignorant."

"As your friend, the right thing for me to do is talk you out of this before it's too late."

"A few minutes ago, I took a selfie with him outside and put on Facebook that my hunky boyfriend and I are at the taproom to celebrate his first day as librarian and finally having him in town after dating long-distance."

"So, too late, then," Evie said. "Did you really say *hunky*?"

"Yes, because he is."

This time Mallory *literally* facepalmed. "Someday you'll learn to wade into trouble slowly so you can get out if you need to instead of cannonballing straight into the deep end."

Actually, she probably wouldn't because her brain was wired to cannonball first and worry about how deep the water was later. She was better than she used to be because she'd learned some coping mechanisms, but an urge to help another person if they were distressed was often her undoing.

And Mallory knew that, but Molly didn't take offense. The Suttons sometimes got exasperated with her, but they loved and accepted her.

"Okay," Mallory said. "We'll go along with this because the only other option is making the poor guy a town joke before he's even unpacked all of his boxes, but I hope you keep it short."

"So, like a couple of weeks?" Evie asked.

"We didn't set an end date," Molly admitted.

"Did you actually set parameters about *anything*?" Mallory asked.

"Yes," Molly said, rolling her eyes. "He has to be my plus-one for Gwen's wedding."

"Molly!" Evie held up her hands. "That's over a month away."

"We have to make people think he's in a great, committed relationship until they get used to him. A couple of weeks isn't long enough."

Mallory laughed and headed for the stairs. "When

you and the librarian get married, I better be your maid of honor."

"Matron of honor," Evie corrected, following her sister down the stairs.

"I'm not going to *marry* him," Molly protested, but the Sutton sisters were halfway down the stairs and weren't listening to her.

Callan took a sip of his beer and watched Molly setting a full glass in front of a customer at the other end of the bar, not minding sitting alone for a few minutes after being dragged through the social gauntlet.

She hadn't been wrong about dating her giving him an opportunity to meet a lot of people really quickly.

He really liked watching Molly work. She was obviously comfortable in this environment and with these people, and her personality shone as she moved through the crowd. Even though she'd said it was part-time and she wasn't actually an employee of the taproom, it was obvious the work suited her.

When she'd come back from wherever she'd gone with Mallory and the other blonde woman, Irish had sent his wife to the house to be with her mother and sons and to put her feet up. And the youngest sister—Evie, if he remembered correctly—had disappeared after getting a phone call.

And Molly had stepped up to Callan from the

wrong side of the bar, giving him a sheepish smile. "Do you mind if I help out for a few minutes? Mallory is exhausted and Evie has to run home and help her husband get some antibiotics into their baby because Becca keeps spitting it out. But it won't be for long."

"Of course I don't mind. It must be tough for a family business when the employees are having babies."

"It's okay. They have me to help."

He sipped his beer, wondering if it was just in her nature to help anybody who needed it in any way she could. With the bar, it made sense. They were lifelong friends of hers. But she didn't even know him, yet she'd volunteered to be bound to him by a fake relationship for the foreseeable future.

She returned to check on him several times, though he assured her he was fine. The beer, which Irish told him he and Lane—Evie's husband— brewed in the cellar, was exceptional, and he'd always enjoyed watching people. Especially her, though he didn't tell her that.

"Is there a food menu?" Callan asked once Evie returned and Molly hopped onto the stool next to his.

"They have some snack-type stuff, but not actual meals because that would require more money and staff than they have. But you can have food from the Stonefield House of Pizza delivered here if you want. They have an arrangement."

After some discussion, they discovered they both liked sausage-and-mushroom pizzas and decided to have a medium delivered. He met more people, ate some pizza, talked with Molly and whoever happened to wander by, ate more pizza and got to know Irish a bit. He'd been a cowboy in Montana, which explained the hat and boots, until he'd stopped by to visit Lane on his way to see the ocean and fell in love with Mallory and her two sons. Now he was a part owner of the brewery and they were not far from having a baby.

Even though he was enjoying himself, Callan was an introvert by nature and he'd had a big day. His social battery was drained and all he wanted to do was go home, flop onto the couch and stare at the ceiling in silence for a while.

"I think I'm going to head out," he told Molly, and he had to lean close because the volume in the place went up as the sun went down. But when she started to slide off her stool, he shook his head. "You can stay. You're having a good time, and I can find my way home from here."

"Are you sure? I don't mind leaving."

"I'm sure. And I settled up with Irish while you were in the bathroom a few minutes ago, so that's all set."

She frowned slightly, and then he heard her breath catch when he lowered his face to hers. He didn't want to kiss her in front of everybody, but he was supposed to be her boyfriend, so he had to do *something*. He settled for brushing his lips across her cheek and inhaling the soft scent of her soap or shampoo or whatever it was.

"Thanks for tonight," he said, his mouth close enough to her ear to make her shiver.

"Are you sure you don't want me to leave with you?" she asked again, a hint of color staining her cheeks.

Their gazes locked and he wavered for a few seconds. He was enjoying her company and if they were someplace quieter, he'd probably stay. But he was afraid if they left together, they were going to spend the night together and that would be a disaster. Not the sex—he hoped, anyway—but the effect sleeping together could have on their fake relationship. He was going to have to draw that line in the sand for himself so he didn't forget what they were doing.

"I'm sure. I'll probably see you tomorrow, though."

Stepping out into the chilly night air was a relief, and by the time he'd walked back to his new home, he felt as if he'd regained his footing where Molly was concerned. There was something about being close to her that addled his brain and he was going to have to be careful not to surrender to the utterly inexplicable attraction he felt for her.

He'd only been home about fifteen minutes before his phone signaled a FaceTime call from Rome. "Hey, Rome."

"I only have a few minutes, but how are things?"

"Good. I'm planning to strip some wallpaper off the walls tonight, so that's exciting."

"Don't be an ass. How was your first day as a small-town librarian?

He filled Rome in on everything that had happened in the last twenty-four hours, ending with, "So now I have a fake girlfriend who wears sweaters with mermaids on them."

"You have a *what* now?" Then Rome held up one finger before reaching out of view to where Callan knew his desk phone sat. "Lacey, can you push my next meeting ten minutes, please? Tell them I'm on an urgent call with an international client. Time zones and all that. Thank you."

For Rome to push back business for a personal call was a big deal, so Callan braced himself for the reality of having to say the ridiculous words out loud again.

"Okay, Callan. I know I misheard you, so repeat that last part for me."

"I'm pretending the woman who lives next door, at the funeral home, is my girlfriend so the residents who were surprised their new librarian is not a stern, older woman think I'm a stable, *not*-single guy and have time to get to know me so I don't lose the job I just barely started."

Rome laughed so hard, Callan was tempted to hang up on him. But his friend would only call back and be even worse having gotten under Callan's skin, so he suffered until Rome had himself under control again.

"Is this one of those horror stories where you go to a small town and get replaced by a pod person or something?" Rome asked, shaking his head. "I can't think of anything that sounds less like you than this."

"I could teach Macarena classes at the library."

"Okay, I can't think of *almost* anything that sounds less like you. And thanks for that mental picture I can never unsee."

"I'm not really sure what happened," Callan admitted. "She has this energy and enthusiasm that you just get swept up in. She's like a tornado that lands and spins you around and then leaves you wondering what the hell just happened."

Rome was quiet for a few seconds, the speculation clear in his expression. "I was wrong. There *is* something less like you."

"What's that?"

"The way your face lights up and gets all animated when you talk about this woman."

Callan scoffed. "You should clean your screen or something. You're seeing things."

"Send me a picture of her."

"No."

Rome's gaze flicked away for a few seconds—

presumably to check the time—and then he frowned. "I have to run, but I'm going to be in touch soon. And a lot. I think your life is about to get very interesting."

He disconnected before Callan could tell him he was wrong. His life wasn't *about* to get very interesting.

It already was.

Chapter Five

Two bicycles were reported stolen from Forest Lane yesterday. People, this is a small town. You can't ride them without somebody recognizing them. Stonefield PD asks that you leave them in the town square or in the school parking lot and no questions will be asked. They promise.

—Stonefield Gazette *Facebook Page*

Molly walked into the Perkin' Up Café with her phone in her hand and Callan on her mind—maybe because Callan's face was *on* her screen. He was revamping the library's social media, which included adding Instagram in addition to dusting off the sadly neglected Facebook Page. In addition to some lovely photos of the small brick library, there was a *meet the librarian* photo and she was having a hard time scrolling past it.

Callan looked warm and welcoming against a backdrop of stained glass and books. His smile wasn't broad, but it was real. It made his eyes crinkle a little behind the glasses, and his shoulders were relaxed. It had definitely been taken in the Stonefield Library, but it didn't look like a selfie, which left her wondering who exactly had taken the photo.

The mostly likely candidate was Mrs. Denning, but Molly didn't think it had been her. His expression wouldn't have been so unreserved with the outgoing librarian behind the camera. But who else could it have been?

And why hadn't he asked *her* to take it? She was his pretend girlfriend, after all.

When it was her turn to step up to the counter, Molly looked up at the chalkboard of options, realizing she'd been so engrossed in Callan's picture, she hadn't thought about her order. The man actually had the power to distract her from caffeine. "I don't know what I want."

"You're getting plain coffee. Black. Lukewarm." Chelsea could put a lot of snark into just one look. "And it's *decaf*."

Molly gasped. "You wouldn't."

Chelsea set a small plain cup of black liquid on the counter. "Oh, I already did."

"But why?"

"It's payback because I had to hear about you dating the sexy new librarian from Daphne Fisk."

"Dammit." The real estate agent not only got the best gossip, but was in the café several times a day. Molly should have guessed she'd beat her to it.

"But," Chelsea continued, "as your alleged friend, I know you have *not* been long-distance dating Callan Avery since his first interview, which means something very interesting is going on in your life and you didn't tell me. So, it's small, black and decaffeinated coffees for you until you tell me everything."

"Fine, I'll tell you because there's nothing *alleged* about our friendship. Daphne just gets out of bed earlier than I do." The bell over the door rang, reminding Molly there were other customers in the café. "But I can't tell you right now because people might hear."

Chelsea gave her a sweet smile, and then she pushed the cup closer to Molly's hand. "I understand. Enjoy your decaf."

Molly sighed and picked up the cup. Caffeine was one of the ways she semi-managed her ADHD and decaf wasn't going to get the job done. After she turned to make room for the next customer, Chelsea very pointedly cleared her throat.

Molly groaned and turned back. "You're going to make me pay for this? It's basically brown water."

All she got was another of those deceptively sweet smiles, so Molly put her card in the reader, adding a tip because she couldn't *not*, and then took her fake coffee to a table to send a text message to Chelsea about her fake relationship. If she could type fast enough on her phone, she might be granted some caffeine before she had to leave.

It took five text messages to tell the story, and they weren't short ones. Then she sipped her punishment coffee, shuddering at the lack of creamy sweetness, and waited for a lull in customers so Chelsea could check her phone.

Finally, she watched her friend pick up the phone, and Chelsea's eyes grew wider and wider as she read. By the time she reached the end, her mouth was literally hanging open.

Then she looked across the café to her table. "Molly Cyrs, you *are not*."

Molly winced as the rest of the customers fell silent, their gossip detectors making them perk up like dogs hearing a cheese wrapper.

She shook her head quickly, trying to signal Chelsea not to say anything else out loud. Then Chelsea started typing furiously on her phone and Molly exhaled a sigh of relief.

"She's dating that new librarian," she heard a woman whisper. "For months, I heard. They talked on the *internet*."

Molly rolled her eyes. The woman made an everyday method of communication sound downright salacious.

Then she overheard the word *sexting* and it was probably a good thing her phone vibrated with a response from Chelsea.

Molly Cyrs, you are not.

You said that part out loud already. Huge waste of thumb energy.

Do Mallory and her sisters know?

You, Mal, Gwen and Evie are the only people who know the truth. And Callan and me, of course.

There was a brief pause when another customer entered and Chelsea had to put together a whole line of complicated drinks for an office. Molly might have made her escape while Chelsea was loading them into cardboard carriers since she needed to get on with her day, but she was still hoping to get a replacement coffee that was actually real coffee.

Once the guy juggling multiple cardboard carriers had successfully gotten through the door without dropping any, Chelsea picked up her phone again and started typing.

Molly's phone dinged five times before she could lift it off the table, and she read the rapid-fire text messages.

People only fake date in movies!

He doesn't seem the type.

Wait. How far is the dating going?

How long are you doing this?

I can't believe you didn't tell me and give me the chance to talk you out of it.

Molly laughed, which caught the attention of everybody around her again. One customer looked from Chelsea to Molly and then rolled her eyes as if to say she knew the two were texting instead of talking and it wasn't fair.

She typed her response and hit Send.

I don't have the strength to type anymore because I'm drinking decaf and need to take a nap under the table now.

If you promise to come back after I close and tell me everything, you can toss the decaf and I'll give you whatever you want, on the house.

There was a pause and then another text came through.

Though considering the mess you've gotten yourself into, I'm not sure further caffeinating you is a great idea.

Molly was already on her way to the counter, but she typed as she walked. It's not a mess. It's a strategy.

"You keep telling yourself that," Chelsea said out loud when Molly reached the counter.

"You know caffeine works differently for me, and it helps calm my brain and helps me focus."

"I do know that," Chelsea said. "I also know you ruin the benefits with the sugars and sweetened flavors."

Molly scowled. "You're trying to pop *all* my happy bubbles today."

"He hasn't been in this morning, by the way."

She'd noticed that, but it was too early to know if stopping at the café was going to be part of Callan's regular routine, or if he'd just been looking for a little boost for his first day of work. Or maybe he hadn't unpacked his coffee maker yet, though that seemed unlikely to Molly. Who wouldn't unpack everything necessary to make coffee first?

Of course thinking about Callan made her wonder all over again who had taken his *meet the librarian* photo.

"I might stop by the library and see him," she said.

"Sure. Guys love when their girlfriends interrupt them at work."

"He works at the *public* library. Technically, I wouldn't be interrupting him because his job requires people to go there. I'll check out some books."

"Right after you pay the fines from the last time you checked out a book and thought you returned it, but it was on the back seat floor of your car the whole time?"

"But I did return it. Eventually."

"Not until after you insisted you'd returned it and asked Mrs. Denning if she was embezzling money from the town by charging fraudulent overdue charges," Chelsea reminded her, and Molly winced. Not one of her finer moments.

"I need to stop telling you things."

"And I'll start charging you for the little bit of extra espresso I add to try to counteract the sugar."

"Give me caffeine and I'll come back later and tell you everything in detail," she promised. "*Every* detail."

There really weren't any juicy details to share—yet—but Molly would say whatever she had to in order to get a very large cup of sweet caffeine in her hands.

Callan had spent too much time in the shower, letting the hot water pound muscles stiffened from stripping wallpaper later into the night than he should have, so he wasn't going to have time to stop for a coffee on his way to the library. There was a coffee maker in the office, but it looked at least twenty years old and he'd probably have to do a Google search on how to use the thing.

"So, you're my daughter's boyfriend."

He stopped abruptly when the man who'd spoken stepped from the funeral home's immaculate lawn onto the sidewalk. "I... Good morning. Callan Avery."

He stuck out his hand and the other man shook it. He was tall, which was probably where Molly got it from, but he had sandy-blond hair and a husky build. "Paul Cyrs. I'd say I've heard a lot about you, but apparently I haven't heard the good stuff. It seems so strange the fact you're dating the daughter of a library committee member never came up during the hiring process."

He and Molly really should have thought this through a little more. Or at all, really. "We, um... I didn't want anybody to feel pressured. I apologize for not having introduced myself sooner."

Paul shrugged it off. "Trust me. We're used to surprises whenever Molly's involved. But you should come to dinner tonight. Amanda and I would love the chance to get to know you a little better. Beyond your work credentials, I mean."

There was nothing Callan wanted to do less. "I'd love to."

"Great. I have to take one of the cars in for service, so I have to run, but I'll see you tonight. We generally eat at six, give or take a few minutes."

"I'm looking forward to it," Callan lied, and his

polite smile faded as Paul walked across the lawn toward the long garage.

Even though he was still chafing under the former librarian's supervision, it was a relief to walk into the library. His life might have turned into a very confusing circus, but he always felt at home surrounded by stacks of books. Organized knowledge was as comforting to him as hot cocoa on a frigid day.

It wasn't long after he unlocked the antique wooden doors that Molly walked through them, a very large iced beverage in hand.

"Did you miss the sign on the door?" he asked, because he really wanted to reduce the number of beverages with flimsy lids allowed inside. He'd already seen coffee sloshed on a book and hastily wiped off. And cleaning a smoothie out of the carpet hadn't been fun. He'd like to limit drinks to those in bottles or tumblers with sealable caps.

"I never notice signs. What did it say?"

"None of those," he said, nodding toward the drink. "I probably shouldn't be surprised you're breaking my very first rule, though. Mrs. Denning gave me quite a lecture about you first thing this morning."

"Okay, the embezzlement accusation was regrettable. But to be fair, I *did* apologize to her."

"But you still haven't paid the fines." He tried to sound stern, but amusement ruined the effect. "And she heard you're my girlfriend and now she has concerns that I'll forgive them without making you pay."

Her sigh was dramatic on a cinematic level. "If you go get her, I'll pay them today, right in front of her, so she knows you're not forgiving overdue fines in exchange for sexual favors."

If he'd been eating or drinking anything, he would have choked. "Do you have any filters whatsoever?"

"Not really."

"Okay. Mrs. Denning implied it's a substantial amount of money, though."

"So significant sexual favors than?" When he couldn't think of a response other than *yes, please*, which he didn't say out loud, she laughed. "She knows the fine can't be more than the cost of a replacement copy of the book and it was a mass market paperback, so who's being dramatic now? Seriously. Go get her and I'll pay it."

Callan would rather not have been in the middle of this, but he also didn't want the library committee buying into Mrs. Denning's fears he'd play favorites. Maybe before he agreed to fake date this woman to secure his job, he should have made sure she wasn't blacklisted. Swallowing a chuckle, he went to find the former-and-yet-still-here librarian.

Once Mrs. Denning had pulled up Molly's library card number and calculated how much she owed—which was not as significant an amount as the woman had implied—Molly paid and her account was cleared. Since her card was reinstated and her fines paid in full, Callan hoped that would be the end of it and Mrs. Denning's fears would be laid to rest before they were shared with the library committee. Or anybody else.

"I'll be finishing packing my office if you need anything," Mrs. Denning said to Callan, and he didn't miss the not-so-gracious look she gave Molly before walking away.

"That was a little rude for some overdue books," he muttered.

"To be fair, I've been a pain in her butt for my entire life. When she was warning you off me, did she also tell you about the time my mom got distracted talking to a friend and, left unsupervised, I rearranged half the picture books by color instead of alphabetically?"

He chuckled. "With most people I'd assume they were a child at the time, but with you I'm hoping it wasn't last month."

Laughter burst out of her, and he thought maybe he should hush her a little bit—they were in a library, after all—but he liked hearing it too much to quiet her. "I was five or six. Who took your *meet the librarian* photo?"

She didn't pause or segue or anything—it was as though with no turn signal or tap of the brakes, she jerked the conversational steering wheel into an entirely different direction. "Technically, nobody took the photo, I guess. I was on a video chat with my friend Roman, showing him the library because he'll probably never make the trip from Manhattan and I mentioned I needed to get a photo taken. He took a still shot from the video because, apparently, having my picture taken formally makes me look like a deer with a flashlight pointed at my eyes. Or so he says."

"That explains why you look so warm and personable."

"So I don't *usually* look warm and personable?" he teased.

"You know what I mean. How come you chose Stonefield?"

Another conversational lane change with no warning. "It's not an easy thing to explain."

"That just makes the story more interesting. *Hard to explain* means a lot of fun tangents, you know."

"Okay, though it's probably not as fun a story as you're hoping for. I'm an only child, and I was raised by a young single mother. She worked two jobs, so I spent a lot of time alone."

"And the library was safe and warm," she said.

"Yes. And Mrs. Grant, the librarian, was strict, but she was also kind. She gave me odd jobs to do to keep me busy, and she made sure I did my homework. She helped me find and apply for scholarships. She helped—" His throat closed up and he had to swallow hard past the lump of emotion. "She helped my mom find resources when she got sick. It was

Mrs. Grant who helped me make the funeral arrangements when she died because I was nineteen and had no clue what to do."

"I'm sorry you lost your mom. And Mrs. Grant sounds wonderful. She's why you became a librarian?"

He nodded. "She kept me going through college, when both classes and mourning my mom felt like too much. She was the reference that got me my first job. And she cheered every time I moved to a bigger library or got a promotion. Then I landed in the big city and it felt like a dream come true. She was so happy for me, even though I was too far away to visit more than once or twice a year."

"Is she near here?"

"I grew up in upstate New York, but she passed away last year."

Molly covered his hand with hers. "Callan, I'm so sorry."

"Thank you." He allowed the sorrow to wash over him, acknowledging it without losing himself in it. "It made me think about her a lot, obviously, and what she'd meant to me. And I realized I wouldn't mean that to anybody. In working my way up the promotion ladder, I'd worked my way out of being involved with everything I loved about libraries. I was in an office, administrating. And yes, the administrating is important because without that, there are no services."

"But you wanted to be out front, with the public."

"Yes." He smiled at her. "And it was only a few days after I admitted to myself I was unhappy living in a city and dissatisfied with my job that I saw the posting for a librarian here. It seems like a perfect community for raising a family, too. I can see my kids in this library, and you have good schools."

She wrinkled her nose, but he wasn't sure if it was the mention of kids or the schools. "Our community is far from perfect, but it's a nice town, I guess."

"You guess?" He chuckled. "What keeps you here in Stonefield?"

"Everybody I love is here," she said, as if it was as simple as that. And maybe, for her, it *was* that simple and she'd been born in a place where she'd happily spend the rest of her life, rather than having to hunt for it like so many others did. "Plus, I get free rent."

"As a former resident of a tiny apartment in Brooklyn that I shared with two very messy people and now as a brand-new homeowner, I can appreciate the importance of free rent." And he could throw a conversational curveball of his own. "Did you know I'm coming to family dinner tonight?"

When her eyes widened and a flush crept up her neck, he knew she hadn't known that. "You are?"

"Your father invited me when I ran into him on the sidewalk outside of your... The funeral home."

"You can call it our house. That's what it is, really. Unless we're talking about funerals. Then it's the funeral home, of course, because keeping deceased people in the basement of a regular house gets documentaries made about you."

"Are your parents as…interesting as you?" he asked, trying to imagine having a long conversation with three people who shared Molly's thought process. "I've met your mom, of course, but she didn't do much of the talking and interviews are pretty scripted. And I only talked to your dad for a couple of minutes, aside from this morning."

"My parents are very neurotypical, which is weird because we can't figure out where my ADHD came from."

"Ah." Another piece of the puzzle that was Molly slid into place. Rome's nephew had ADHD, so Callan knew a little about it, but not much. Definitely not enough to keep up with Molly, so he'd have to see what—if anything—the library had on the shelves for reference. He needed to make sure the library had current research on neurodiversity available to the patrons, so as soon as Molly left, he'd make a note to check it out.

"Did he invite you because you're our new neighbor?" she asked, fidgeting with the end of her ponytail.

She sounded almost hopeful that was the case, and he wondered if she was worried about her parents' reaction to them dating. In the moment, she hadn't seemed to be, but he was learning that her leap-first-and-look-later way could complicate things.

"No, he was inviting his daughter's boyfriend to family dinner. I had to fudge an explanation for going through the whole hiring process without mentioning my relationship with you. I said we didn't want them to feel pressured and he seemed to accept that."

"So my mom probably knows already." She sighed and then seemed to shake off any anxiety that news caused her. "My mom's a great cook, but did my dad ask if you have any food allergies or foods that you won't eat?"

"He didn't, but I have no food allergies. And I'm not picky about food, though seafood isn't my favorite. Oh, and I won't eat beets."

"They smell funny."

What a silly thing to send a shot of warmth thought him, Callan thought. "Right? They smell like weird dirt. I've never gotten past the smell enough to try them."

"There won't be beets tonight," she assured him. "And if there's something you don't like, don't worry about not eating it because they're used to it. I'm super picky because I don't like some smells, and I have issues with textures sometimes."

"Do you like pasta?" he asked, even though it didn't matter because they weren't *really* dating, so food compatibility was irrelevant.

"I love pasta, but mostly with creamy sauces. I don't really like red sauces because they have little bits of stewed tomatoes and I don't like mushy bits, so on spaghetti night I just put lots of butter and parmesan cheese on the noodles. Do you want me to text you what Mom's planning to make tonight?"

"Your dad was on his way to get a car serviced, so you might want to start with telling her I'm coming," he said. "And you can surprise me."

Everything about her seemed to take him by surprise, so why should dinner be any different?

When a woman with three kids walked in, followed by two older ladies, he nodded his head toward the drink in her hand, and she blushed.

"Fine, I'll take my drink outside," she said. "But I'll see you for dinner tonight."

She exchanged a few words with one of the older women on her way out, and Callan didn't miss the approving looks all three of the patrons sent his way. Apparently Molly had been right about dating her giving him some instant credibility with the community, which was good because it had been a wild ride so far.

And tonight he was having dinner with her parents. At least it was worth it.

Chapter Six

Town hall is looking for volunteers to help with annual planting in the town square. If you're interested in helping Stonefield look its best, give them a call or visit the town's Facebook Page for more information. Anybody who shows up and plants flowers will receive their choice of a free beverage from the Perkin' Up Café or a free beer from Sutton's Place Brewery & Tavern! (If you're under 21, we recommend the café.)

—Stonefield Gazette *Facebook Page*

After leaving the library, Molly took her time walking home. Her mom refused to even try to understand the effect caffeine had on ADHD brains, and Molly wasn't in the mood to listen to a lecture about the extra-large cup in her hand. Not until she'd sucked every last drop through the straw and tossed the cup into one of the garbage cans around the park did she finally head home.

Molly had an office on the first floor. It was right next to her dad's huge office, so she had to keep it meticulously neat in case the door was open when her father was escorting clients through. Luckily, the fact that hers was roughly the size of a walk-in closet meant a more minimalist approach to clutter. It also meant she spent as little time as possible in it.

Before confining herself to her office closet, she needed to find out if her dad had informed her mom they were having company for dinner. And the big question—how did her mother feel about her daughter secretly dating their new librarian through the process of hiring him? Molly had never shared a lot about her personal life, but Amanda and Paul had discussed the candidates several times over dinner and she hadn't said anything.

Molly wasn't surprised to find her mother upstairs in her office. Amanda Cyrs knew what she was getting into when she married a third-generation funeral director, but she was happiest in the room she'd claimed as her own many years ago.

She also wasn't surprised to see that her mother was holding two paint chips against an already beautiful lavender wall. Redecorating the office was

Amanda's favorite hobby, and Molly didn't blame her at all. The entire downstairs of the home and all of the exterior were immaculately kept in rigidly neutral colors. The furniture was elegant and the decorations tasteful. Her father's office was the same, as that was where he met with people about making funeral arrangements. Even the second and third floors, which were the family's living space, were somewhat bland. Her dad wasn't very adventurous when it came to aesthetics.

But Amanda's office on the third floor could be whatever she wanted it to be, and it changed often.

"Mom, you love that color. You said it was more soothing than the mint. Why don't you change the throw pillows and stuff instead of repainting?"

"I was just looking," she said, and Molly laughed because she always said that right before she repainted. "Your father dropped the car off for service, and now he's downstairs if you're looking for him."

"Oh no." Molly frowned, wondering if she'd missed news in the community. *Downstairs* didn't mean the first floor, but the extensive finished basement where the necessary work of preparing the deceased for their funerals took place.

"He's just cleaning and doing some inventory," her mother assured her. "But while you're here, I talked to Laura Thompson earlier and what is this I hear about you dating Callan Avery?"

That certainly hadn't taken long. The only surprise was that she'd heard the gossip from a friend and not her own husband. "Yeah. We've been talking online since his first interview and it's a lot easier now that he lives next door."

Her mother's gaze sharpened, homing in on her, and Molly forced herself not to fidget. "And you've never mentioned it in all this time?"

"He didn't want you to feel pressured to hire him."

Her mom made that sound that meant *I'm not sure I believe you, but okay.* "And what if he hadn't gotten the job? What would have happened then?"

That was a good question Molly didn't have an answer to. "I... I was pretty sure you'd pick him. I mean, he's *very* qualified and personable and passionate about small community libraries."

"But what if we hadn't?"

Molly was pretty sure her mom was trying to lead her into some kind of conversational trap, but she couldn't see it. "Then Callan and I would have kept talking online for a while, but it probably wouldn't have worked out in the long run."

"You need to start taking your future more seriously, Molly. Talking online, as you say, isn't going to get you settled down."

And there it was—*the look*. The look that said her mother was so disappointed and annoyed and wished Molly had never been born. That she wished she'd had some other kid who could be like other kids.

No.

This was the wiring of her brain lying to her—the chemicals in her brain taking the slightest of admonitions and amplifying it into a total rejection of her.

It was exhausting to hold that in check, like trying to rein in runaway horses. But even though she had to recognize the feeling, examine it and set it aside almost constantly, it still wasn't as exhausting as her teen years, when the emotional horses ran unchecked until her stagecoach crashed and burned. One day in her senior year, she'd been on the internet instead of doing her homework, going from quiz to quiz to find out which animated princess she was or what her perfect vacation destination would be. And she'd stumbled across a quiz that told her she probably had ADHD and should consult a doctor.

Naturally she'd gone to her parents. Her father said ADHD was a thing made up by parents who couldn't control their kids and didn't want it to be their fault. Her mother said she couldn't have ADHD because she was perfectly capable of sitting still when she wanted to. And her doctor relied on input from her parents and told her cut more sugar out of her diet.

But she *knew* with her whole soul that she'd found the answer to the question of why she couldn't do things like everybody else in her life seemed to do them. She'd researched everything she could about how her neurodiverse brain worked, and she learned coping skills and methods of getting things done.

Once she was an adult she'd changed doctors, of course. She had a diagnosis and sometimes she relied on medication to get her through challenges that required a little more executive function than usual.

Her parents had accepted the diagnosis, but they still didn't really understand it. Or her. And they never seemed to have time to read the articles or watch the videos she forwarded to them. Once they'd done the difficult duty of getting her through high school, they'd mostly given up. As long as Molly did her job, they were settled into a tired, slightly exasperated *that's just Molly* place.

It had been a long, emotionally brutal road for Molly to get to where she was now—able to accept and sometimes even embrace her neurodiversity—but her parents still had the ability to get under her skin.

"I *am* settled down, Mom. I'm doing exactly what I want to be doing."

"You know what I mean."

Yes, she did. Molly needed to marry a nice man who would provide for the children they were supposed to have. She fought the urge to roll her eyes at her mother, who had surprisingly old-fashioned ideas for somebody born in the late sixties.

And she was never having kids, though she hadn't told her parents about that decision yet.

"I only came up to ask you if Dad told you he invited Callan to dinner tonight."

That got her mom's attention. Her eyes narrowed

and her lips got that pinched look Molly liked to imagine was Amanda's way of holding back a long string of curse words.

"I saw him briefly, but I had some things to run by him and then he said he knew there was something he meant to tell me, but he forgot what it was. But I'm disappointed he apparently knew you two were dating before I did if he already invited him over."

"I didn't tell him." Molly held up her hand as if swearing an oath. "I was going to tell you together, but I guess the gossip mill acted faster than I thought it would, and then Dad bumped into Callan outside this morning."

After a final sniff to show her displeasure at feeling like the last to know, Amanda shook it off and sat at her desk. "What should I make? What does Callan like?"

That was a very good question. She had an idea of what he *didn't* like, but she hadn't asked him what he *did* like. She'd assume pasta, since he asked her about it, but then meats and sauces were an unknown. "He's not picky. He doesn't really like seafood or beets, though."

"There goes the shrimp and pickled beets salad I was going to start with." Molly's horror, which wasn't even all about Callan's tastes, must have shown on her face because her mom laughed. "I'm kidding. I like shrimp and beets and I still would never."

"Even Dad wouldn't eat that and he eats anything."

"I think a pork roast, with potatoes and my home-made applesauce, with a garden salad and some veggies and rolls. It's a good meal, with enough stuff to pick around any dislikes without leaving the table hungry."

Molly felt a pang of guilt over her mother going to so much trouble for a meet-the-boyfriend dinner when he wasn't *really* her boyfriend. But she really liked her mom's pork roast, so she wasn't going to try to talk her out of it.

Then she realized her mother probably knew more about Callan than she did, thanks to the interview process, and had to stifle a nervous giggle. It was going to be fine, she told herself. Library committees didn't ask for the kind of information a girlfriend would know, so she'd be able to bluff her way through it. And hopefully Callan could, too. Very *worst*-case scenario, her parents would have to be brought into the ruse, but she wanted to avoid that at all costs. Their positions in the town would make that uncomfortable for them. And she'd be able to feel their judgment weighing on her like a super-heavy black shawl draped over her. She definitely didn't want them to find out.

She and Callan just had to smile, lie their asses off and eat pork roast.

The first dinner with a new girlfriend's parents was always excruciatingly awkward. Callan had thought having already met them both, as well as the fact Molly was his *fake* girlfriend, would take some of the pressure off, but he'd been wrong.

The dinner was still excruciating, but now having to lie to Paul and Amanda was the cherry on top of the awkward sundae.

The only blessing was that Molly had met him on the front porch as the oven timer sounded, so he hadn't been left alone with Paul to make pre-dinner small talk. After shaking Paul's hand and saying hello to Amanda, they'd gone straight to the table.

"Are you close with your family?" Paul asked after a few minutes, and Callan froze with his water glass halfway to his mouth. So they were diving straight into the deep end, then.

"We'd love to know more about you on a personal level since we didn't delve into that during the interview process," Amanda added, and then she leveled a pointed look at her daughter. *"Obviously."*

Molly's face flushed and she looked down at her plate, moving a cherry tomato around with the tip of her fork. He thought it was a big reaction for such a small—and admittedly deserved—jab, but he didn't know much about mother-daughter relationships. Maybe this was something ongoing between them.

"It was just my mom and me," he told her parents. "We were very close, but she passed away between my first and second years of college, so I don't have any family."

Even though they thought he was dating their daughter and would probably want to know everything about him, he really hoped they wouldn't ask about his father. The jerk had turned out to be married and he'd turned his back on Hope Avery when she told him she was pregnant. That was all Callan knew, since he'd never broken the seal on the envelope his mother had given him before she died because that was all he cared to know. If he was backed into a conversational corner, though, and had to confess he didn't know who his father was, he'd have to suffer their pity. Or even worse, they'd start talking about DNA databases and genealogy sites as if he hadn't decided for himself that he had zero need to look for the man. He wasn't the kind of man Callan would want in his life, and sharing some DNA wasn't enough to change that.

"I'm sorry you lost your mother," Amanda said in a much softer tone than she'd used with Molly a moment ago. "Stonefield is a wonderful community, so hopefully you'll make your home here and make good friends."

"Thank you. That's the plan." *Literally.* Molly tried to turn her laughter into a cough, and he thought about nudging her ankle with his under the table. "I do have a very good friend back in the city. Roman is almost like a brother to me."

"That's lovely," Amanda said. "Have you met him yet, Molly?"

"No, not yet. I hope to soon, though. Maybe."

"Rome's in finance in Manhattan," Callan said, hoping to smooth over Molly's hesitant response. "He's a workaholic and not an easy man to pin down for more than a few minutes outside of his work."

"Are you childhood friends?" Amanda asked.

"No, ma'am. We didn't meet until I was working in the city—or we thought we hadn't met, actually. We were introduced through a mutual acquaintance who knew he was from upstate, too. It turns out we're from towns not far from each other and we played each other in high school."

"Oh, did you play sports?" Paul asked, visibly taking more of an interest in the conversation.

"Chess, actually. I tried out for baseball, but I wasn't able to overcome my aversion to very hard, very fast balls flying at my face."

"I belonged to the chess club in middle school," Molly said.

"Until you realized you'd actually have to play chess," Amanda said with a shake of her head.

Callan wasn't sure he wanted to know, but he had to ask. "Why did you join the chess club if you didn't want to play chess?"

"A boy," Molly confessed. "I thought I could just hang out with the rest of them and be like his personal chess cheerleader, but it turns out that's not really a thing. And you have to be quiet, so they can concentrate or whatever. So yes, I was a member of the middle school chess club for sixteen minutes."

The laughter around the table eased the last of the getting-to-know-you tension and the rest of dinner passed with easy, casual conversation. They talked mostly about libraries and books, of course, since the Cyrs family business wasn't really a subject for the dinner table. Amanda told him all about the best places to shop, including Dearborn's Market for groceries and Sutton's Seconds for almost everything else.

"It's Mallory's mom's thrift shop," Molly told him.

"And Chelsea at the Perkin' Up Café makes all kinds of fancy coffee drinks if you're into that kind of thing," Paul added.

"I've been there and she does make very good coffee," Callan agreed. "That's where Molly and I met...for coffee. That's where we met for coffee yesterday before my first day of work."

He wasn't very good at this, and he belatedly realized he probably should have come up with an excuse to decline family dinner invitations until he and Molly had had time to come up with some backstory for their relationship.

"That's also where we actually met," Molly said lightly. "When he was in town for his interview. We exchanged info, started talking and here we are."

Yes, here they were. With him overcomplicating and overthinking this thing, which would probably lead to them giving everything away. He wasn't sure if their deception was serious enough to cost him his job, but it would certainly cause him to be humiliated if they were discovered. And in a town like this, that sort of thing could linger for a long time. Generations, even.

Molly's toes nudged his ankle and Callan realized he'd been glaring at his empty plate. He took a breath and fixed a pleasant smile on his face. Then his gaze locked with hers and he instantly felt lighter and more relaxed. They could do this.

Despite the shot of confidence, it was still a relief to thank her parents for the lovely dinner and escape out the front door with Molly. He breathed in the fresh air for a few moments, calming himself, before he realized Molly was looking up at him. Her eyes were questioning and she'd caught her bottom lip between her teeth, and he realized she was anxious.

"That went pretty well," he said, and her teeth released her lip as she smiled up at him.

"At least my mom's a good cook. No matter how awkward the conversation gets, it's almost worth it for her homemade applesauce."

"I've never had homemade before. Now I'm ruined for store-bought applesauce forever."

"She cans massive amounts of it, so I might be able to sneak you a jar or two," she said as they walked down the steps and down the walkway.

"So you live over the garage?" he asked, nodding toward the long row of closed garage doors.

"Come on and I'll show you."

He'd asked out of curiosity and a need to fill the silence more than a desire to actually go upstairs with her, but in what he was learning was typical Molly fashion, as soon as the thought popped into her head, she was moving. It was either follow her and get the tour or stand alone in the yard until she realized he wasn't behind her and came back. So he followed her.

Her apartment wasn't huge, especially since it had slanted ceilings thanks to the steep pitch of the roof. But the walls were painted a very pale and cheerful yellow, and the decor was as eclectic and colorful as he'd expect from a woman who wore a mermaid sweater. It somehow managed to be both fun *and* calming, and he wondered if it was possible to be in a bad mood in her space.

She didn't show him her bedroom, which he glimpsed through the open door at the far end of the apartment, and he thought that was probably for the best.

"So this is it," she said, waving her hand at the open-concept space around them.

"It's so much lighter than I expected," he said. "It's very *you*, and I mean that as a compliment."

"Thank you," she chirped with a bright smile.

And then Callan was frozen in a moment where, if they'd really been dating, he would have moved in for a kiss. If she was really his girlfriend, he'd be wondering if she'd genuinely just wanted to show him her place, or if she'd brought him up here to move things along in a physical sense.

But she wasn't his girlfriend, and she had simply answered his curiosity about her apartment with an offer of a tour. There was nothing else on the table because their relationship wasn't real, and it was time for him to go before he forgot that very important fact.

"I should probably get going," he told her, already backing toward the door. "Dinner was delicious, so I appreciate the invitation, and I'll see you tomorrow."

"I'm sure you'll be getting a lot of dinner invites, so I'm glad you liked it. Good night, Callan."

It wasn't a long walk across their yard, around the fence, and across his yard to get to his front door, but it was plenty of time for her words to run through his head several times. *I'm sure you'll be getting a lot of dinner invites.* Because he lived next door and Amanda thought he and Molly were a couple, so why *wouldn't* he want to eat with them?

After closing the door behind him, he turned and rested his head against the wood. What had he gotten himself into, and how was he supposed to get out of it without losing his job?

And even worse, did he actually *want* to get out of it?

Chapter Seven

*Don't forget Mother's Day is this Sunday!
Dearborn's Market has everything you need to
make breakfast in bed for that special woman
in your life. They also have a variety of cards,
cakes and boxed chocolates to make the day
extra special for her. If you want to give her
flowers that will last, stop by Wilson's Garden
Center before 3:00 p.m. on Saturday, or Bob
will have flowers that won't last on sale at the
gas station for those last-minute shoppers.*
                    —Stonefield Gazette *Facebook Page*

"Sit down for a minute."

This was one of the rare times Molly was in the
taproom and did *not* want to sit with the woman who

was like a second mother to her, but Ellen Sutton had spoken. Molly sat.

She was across the table from Ellen and her best friend, Laura Thompson—Evie's mother-in-law—and Molly felt their eyes on her like an interrogator's spotlight. They were very smart ladies who'd known Molly her entire life, and in the time it took her to put her butt in the chair, she reminded herself to keep it simple. Having been talking online since Callan's interview wasn't that big of a lie, but if her anxiety pushed her to word-vomit to fill silence, she was going to end up telling too many tall tales to track.

"You haven't sat still long enough to talk to in ages," Ellen said.

"We want to hear all about you and Callan," Laura added. Of course they did. "I finally got a chance to chat with him at the library today and he seems to have survived his first full week without Mrs. Denning."

He'd actually had a much better week without her than last week, when she'd been looking over his shoulder, but Molly kept that to herself. She was much more curious about what Callan and Laura had talked about. Hopefully he hadn't looked as anxious about their story as he had during their dinner with her parents.

"He's still settling in," Molly said. "But he really likes it here. No regrets or anything."

"I can't believe none of the girls told me you were

seeing our new librarian," Ellen said. "Or not seeing, I guess, since you were chatting online until recently."

"We didn't tell anybody because my mom was on the hiring committee and how that might look." Maybe she could distract them away from her Callan situation with one of their favorite topics of conversation. "I saw Becca the other day. She's getting so big!"

Laura's face lit up. "Isn't she? It's hard to believe she's almost four months old already."

"It goes by so fast," Ellen said, and the two women exchanged a sappy look that made Molly smile.

Two best friends sharing a grandchild was the sweetest thing, she thought. They'd all assumed it would happen when Evie and Lane—who were high school sweethearts—had gotten married after college. Then Lane's dad had died, they'd gotten divorced and Evie had left Stonefield. Now, years later, Ellen and Laura reveled in finally sharing a granddaughter.

As she'd hoped, Laura and Ellen got sidetracked talking about the baby and showing her pictures on their phones. It killed enough time so Molly didn't feel bad when she pushed back her chair and stood.

"It was nice to finally get to chat, but I should see if they need help. It's pretty busy." It really wasn't, but there were enough customers to make it believable. She just wanted to get away from their table before they circled back to Callan.

"Did they get the truth out of you?" Evie asked when they crossed paths at the bar.

"Nope. I distracted them by asking about your daughter."

Evie laughed. "That's guaranteed to work. They're here tonight because Lane talked them into it so he could have some quiet time with Becca. Between Ellen and Laura, they hardly ever put her down."

"On the plus side, you don't have to pay for baby-sitting."

"True. Though we'll see what happens when Mallory pops."

"When Mallory what?" Mallory asked, making Molly jump. She hadn't seen her come in, and she had Gwen with her.

While they hadn't talked about it directly, Molly had heard from Mallory that Gwen's opinion of the save-Callan's-job ruse hadn't been positive. But Molly hadn't really thought it would be. Embracing a wild idea that hadn't been thought through wasn't really Gwen's style.

"When you pop out that kid," Evie said, nodding at her belly. "I was telling Molly I might lose my free babysitter when your little one's born."

"You'll still have Laura," Molly pointed out. When Mallory's baby was born, Ellen would be the grandmother, but Laura would be the great-aunt, so Becca would still be her number one.

Gwen shook her head. "You know those two. They've already decided Evie and Mal's babies are going to be the best of friends as well as cousins, so they're going to have them in a playpen *together*."

Irish appeared at their end of the bar, his eyes on his wife. "I thought you were going to relax with your feet up."

"I *was* relaxing with my feet up, but I was getting tired of listening to the boys yell at their friends over their gaming headsets and Gwen came over, and... I can't sit with my feet up for another month and a half, Irish. I know this is your first baby, but it's my third, so you need to trust that I'm listening to my body."

Molly could tell he wanted to argue—he was so anxious about the baby—but then he gave Mallory a warm smile. "Okay. Do you want a water?"

"In a few minutes. We'll probably sit with Mom and Laura and make Evie wait on us."

"Good luck with that," Evie said, and they all laughed as Irish went back to his other customers.

"Okay," Mallory said, turning to Molly. "It's been like a week and half since you started this nonsense. What's going on?"

Molly shrugged. "Nothing but what I told you. We're pretending to date and it's going well. People are warming up to him at the library and I'll have a date to Gwen's wedding. As planned."

"And that's it?" Evie asked, clearly disappointed.

She wasn't alone. Fake dating wasn't nearly as exciting as Molly had imagined it would be. So far it consisted of walking to the café, where they took turns paying for their morning coffee. She'd pop into the library. And she'd gone shopping at the market with him once.

So far, she was highly caffeinated and reading more books, but as an adventure, pretending to be a girlfriend was a bit of a letdown.

"All three of us are worried about this, you know," Gwen said. "You don't do things in moderation. Everything you do, you do with your whole heart and this…this can't be done that way, Molly. Not without it being a disaster."

Molly's skin tingled with heat, and she tried not to let it show on her face. There was something about concern coming from Gwen that sounded more like judgment or condemnation than when it came from Mallory. Maybe it was because she'd been gone for so long, but Evie had been, too. More likely it was that Gwen was the oldest, and she and Molly just had radically different personalities.

"Everything's going according to plan," she said, trying not to sound defensive.

"Speaking of," Mallory said, nodding her toward the door.

Molly turned to see Callan walking in, and her pulse quickened. He scanned the room and when his gaze finally landed on her, a warm smile softened the lines of his face. Heat rushed through her and she couldn't help smiling back as he started toward her.

"Sure," Gwen said. "Totally according to plan."

Callan felt the already familiar jolt of warmth and anticipation he felt whenever he saw Molly, which was probably why it took a moment to realize she was with Mallory and Gwen Sutton, and Evie was there, too. So much for his hope of sitting at the bar, reading a book and stealing moments with Molly in between customers.

After closing the library, he'd eaten a light dinner and spent some time sanding living room walls he was prepping for paint. He wanted that done as quickly as possible because he'd had to move the TV and pretty much everything else into his bedroom until he was finished. But he'd only worked a couple of hours before he couldn't resist stepping outside to see if the lights were on in Molly's apartment. It looked dark, so he'd showered and walked to the tavern. He could tell himself he wanted a Friday-night beer after a long workweek, but he really just wanted to see Molly.

And what was the point of pretending they were dating if they weren't seen in public together beyond morning coffees and a trip to the market? It was a strategic move, really. Or it had seemed that way until pretty much all the important women in

Molly's life turned their heads to look at him when he walked in.

"Now, see, I like a guy who brings a book to a bar," Gwen said. "There should be more reading in bars."

Callan slid his arm around Molly's waist and kissed her cheek for the benefit of the other customers. He felt her shiver when his lips touched her skin and his body tightened in response. He had to clear his throat before he could speak. "I thought Molly might be working, so I'd need something to keep me occupied while she was busy."

"It's too bad Nichole isn't here tonight," Mallory said. "She's always reading and you guys could probably talk about books for hours."

Judging by the way Molly scowled, he surmised that Nichole was a bar patron, and he had to admit Molly did fake jealousy well. So well he thought veering the conversation away from Nichole seemed like a good idea. "That reminds me, does this town have a book club?"

"Not really," Molly said. "There used to be one that met at the library, but Ronnie said something was an allegory and Suzie said she was using allegory wrong and it escalated. Ronnie threw her large fountain drink at Suzie and missed, and she ended up soaking half a shelf of European history books with orange soda. Mrs. Denning canceled book club *and* Ronnie's library card that day."

The idea that somebody had brought a large fountain drink into the library made Callan's skin crawl. "That's why one doesn't bring food or beverages into a library."

Molly rolled her eyes. "If you're going to sit and talk about allegories—or *not* allegories—in boring books for two hours, sometimes *one* gets thirsty."

He chuckled. "If you're going to talk to me about allegories for two solid hours, my beverage better be alcoholic."

She gasped. "Oh! We should host a book club here! And call it something fun, like… Books and Beer."

"Books & Brews," Callan said.

Molly slapped his arm as her face lit up. "Yes! Books & Brews. That's perfect."

The way she couldn't restrain herself when she was excited was starting to grow on him. Not the slapping so much, but it wasn't as if it had been a hard hit. She just had these bursts of *I need your attention right now* and that was how she got it.

"Gwen!" Before he could do anything to stop it, Molly waved her friend over. "We want to have a book club that meets here and we'll call it Books & Brews."

"Do not even *think* about using one of my books," Gwen told her. "I mean it."

Callan knew who Gwen Sutton was. The hold list at his old library in New York had been out of control when it was announced her first book, *A Quak-*

ing of Aspens, was being turned into a movie. It had also been the choice for one of the book clubs he'd been in at the library and the conversation had been lively, but he didn't think he'd share that little tidbit of information right now.

Mrs. Denning had filled him in on their famous local author, of course. Apparently she'd moved away for many years. Some said it was out of shame for using the residents of Stonefield as fodder for her book—apparently Mrs. Bickford thought the character who'd died in a horribly tragic accident on the page was her son, Tony. And others said she'd left because she was sick of explaining to the people of her hometown that the book was a work of fiction and none of them were in it. When she'd come back to town to help her family open the brewery after her father died, she'd fallen in love and stuck around, but old annoyances died hard, apparently.

Molly was bouncing up and down on the balls of her feet. "We can put a box on the end of the bar and at the library introducing the book club and asking for suggestions for the inaugural Books & Brews read."

"I wonder if Irish and Lane could brew up a special edition beer," Mallory added.

Callan was on a runaway train—the Cyrs & Sutton Railroad, he thought—and it was going to derail if he didn't regain control of the situation. "Asking for suggestions is going to end up with a list of as many books as people signed up and some of those people will feel put out their book wasn't picked."

"I don't know," Molly said, frowning at him. "People will be more excited if they get a say."

"I *do* know. I know book clubs because I'm a librarian."

"Yeah, well, Gwen's an author. Tons of book clubs have invited her to visit them."

"I want no part of this," Gwen said, holding up both hands as she backed away. "But Callan's right."

Molly rolled her eyes. "Fine. But you're not the sole picker of the book. We'll decide together so you don't pick one of those super-boring book club books."

Callan struggled to keep a straight face. "I'll do my best not to pick a book club book for book club."

When she realized what she'd said, she laughed and he laughed along with her. He loved that she could laugh at herself like that and then move on.

"No nonfiction. No dust bowls. Nothing bad can happen to animals. And definitely no male protagonists looking at their belly buttons."

"I'm sorry, no *what*?"

"She means navel-gazing," Mallory said. "Sometimes her mouth moves faster than her brain and if she's missing a word, just fills it in with something close. We're pretty fluent in Molly-ese."

Callan nodded and smiled at Molly. "Okay, what about *female* protagonists looking at their belly buttons?"

Molly crossed her arms. "Now I don't know if you're talking about navel-gazing or if you have a fetish we don't know about yet."

"Speaking of fetishes," Mallory said. "Did you come to an agreement on the exhibitionist thing?"

"I'm not an exhibitionist," Callan said, because he didn't see any way out of it. "Nor am I a voyeur."

"No comment on belly buttons?" Molly asked, giving him a look that could only be called saucy.

"While I might occasionally be guilty of navel-gazing, I do *not* have a belly button fetish. And before you ask, no, I'm not going to tell you what—if any—fetishes I do have."

"I guess she'll have to find out for herself," Mallory said, and then she pressed her hand to her mouth before looking around to make sure nobody was paying attention to them. "Sorry," she whispered. "Sometimes I forget you're not actually a couple."

Sometimes he forgot, too. Not for very long, but he liked when that happened. He liked it less when he remembered. "I guess we must be good at it."

Mallory's eyebrow arched. "Pretending or being a couple?"

He and Molly both laughed, but he thought they both sounded as fake as their relationship. And also, the C&SRR train was running away from him again.

"Back to the books," he said, trying to get them back on track. "We'll pick one and then I'll put in the interlibrary loan requests to get enough copies.

"It's too bad we can't use one of Gwen's books," Molly said. "Her publisher sends her boxes of author copies."

"No," Gwen called across the taproom, and Callan realized they'd all turned to look at her when Molly said that.

"I'm going to go sit with Mom and Ellen for a few minutes," Mallory said, giving Irish a wave before walking away.

Callan thought maybe he was going to get a minute alone with Molly, but Evie called her name and waved her over to a table by the back of the room, where the taproom was separated from the stairs down to the brewing cellar by a glass wall. A lot of personal and brewing memorabilia that had belonged to the Sutton sisters' dad was hung on the other side of it, and family photos hung behind the bar. There were also shelves of glasses with the taproom's logo and the regulars had their names etched into the glass. As he slid onto a stool, he wondered how many times a person had to visit to get their own glass.

Irish set a coaster in front of him. "What did you get them all riled up about?"

"I asked if there was a book club in town." Callan shook his head. "Somehow that led to a plan to host Books & Brews events here in the taproom."

"Huh."

"Although none of the people involved in the discussion actually own the place, so I guess somebody will have to run that up the ladder."

Irish chuckled. "Well, there's whose name is on the legal documents, and then there's who runs the place. It's very much a family business in all the best—and worst—of ways."

"They seem like a force to be reckoned with."

"There's a reason why, when we were talking about Case's bachelor party, the most popular option was renting a bunch of hotel rooms, turning our phones off, hanging do-not-disturb signs and sleeping for a solid twenty-four hours."

"Sounds like a helluva party."

Irish nodded and pulled a glass off the rack. "What'll you have?"

Chapter Eight

*Big news! Sutton's Place Brewery & Tavern is
teaming up with the library to host Books &
Brews, a fun book club where beverages are
not only permitted, but encouraged! Mr. Avery
and Molly Cyrs have narrowed the inaugural
book down to three finalists, so head on over
to the Stonefield Library's Facebook Page to
vote for your choice.*
　　　　　　　—Stonefield Gazette *Facebook Page*

"**D**on't you think it's a little weird that we've been
fake dating for almost two weeks and I haven't seen
the inside of your house?" Molly peered over the top
of the circulation desk to see Callan better. "I want
a job where I get to read magazines."

"It's an industry publication, reviewing upcoming titles so I can choose where to spend the book budget." He looked up her and smiled. "But yeah, I get paid to read this magazine."

"But don't you think it's weird?"

"Reading reviews? Not really."

"No, that I haven't been inside your house."

"Trust me when I tell you the inside of my house is *not* something worth seeing right now. I'm probably not the first man to come to the realization that do-it-yourself renovation isn't as easy as it sounds."

"Have you ever done it before?"

He laughed. "I patched a hole in the wall of my first apartment and I replaced a faucet once. And I watch a lot of YouTube videos."

"Clearly you're qualified to renovate an entire house, then." She laughed, shaking her head.

"Is this where you tell me you secretly have mad carpentry, plumbing and electrical skills and you turned the space over the garage into a cute apartment all by yourself?" He grinned. "I hope?"

"Sorry. I did try to help my dad fix the shed once and I was hammering the nail for him and a butterfly went by and…well, I learned some really good curse words that day and his thumbnail was dark purple for a while."

"He let you hammer while he held the nail?"

She didn't blame him at all for looking skeptical and maybe slightly horrified. "In his defense, I was pretty young. I don't think they'd given up hope yet. What are you working on now?"

"I've got the living room walls almost ready to paint. I just need to pick a color. The natural lighting isn't great, so it'll have to be light. But not white. I haven't decided yet."

"We should steal my mother's paint chips. She has an entire collection because she paints her office more often than I paint my nails."

"She might not like us stealing her paint chips, then. It sounds like she uses them a lot."

Molly waved her hand. "We'll give them back."

"Okay, so borrowing. Not stealing." He chuckled when she rolled her eyes at him. "But if you want to come over after work tonight, I'll give you a tour and you can weigh in on the paint color."

"Oh, fun!" She bounced on the balls of her feet.

"Molly." He looked as if he was already regretting the offer and she forced herself to try to look serious. "My living room is not… It's not a mermaid sweater."

"But it could be, Callan. It could be."

And then she blew him a kiss and practically ran out of the library before he could start setting ground rules for the paint color choices. His paint chips were probably a bunch of different shades of beige, ecru and cream. Or maybe they were all shades of each other. She didn't even know.

Her mother was in her office and wasn't on the

phone or typing, so Molly was already crossing the threshold as she knocked twice against the jam. "You busy, Mom?"

"Do you think Chelsea gets a discount or some kind of wholesale price on coffee things?"

"I don't know. I can ask if there's something specific you want to know."

Amanda sighed. "I'd like to get a larger coffee urn, but decorative, so during the longer visitations, people can help themselves. But I've been pricing them and they're so expensive."

"I don't think she has anything like that, but she might have a supplier who does. I'll ask her." She reached into her bag and pulled out her notebook to jot the task down. She didn't put a star next to it, though. Her mother had been considering an updated coffee urn for two years. "Can I borrow your paint chip collection?"

Her mother actually clapped her hands together. "You're finally getting rid of that awful yellow?"

A flush of resentment and shame heated Molly's skin. She loved the color of her apartment, but Amanda had urged her to go with a creamier, less yellow tone and she'd never gotten over the fact Molly hadn't listened to her.

But she was here on Callan's behalf, so instead of telling her mother to never mind and going off to vent her frustration through some physical activity, she forced herself to stay calm.

"Callan can't decide on a color for his living room, so I said maybe we could borrow your chips for tonight. I'm going to go over and help him decide."

"Not yellow," she muttered, but then her face brightened. "I'll go with you. Three opinions are better than two. We can get a consensus."

"I..." She wasn't sure what to say to that. She wasn't wrong, but would Callan mind?

Probably not, she decided. He'd made it clear he needed all the renovation help he could get. Her mother wasn't very handy with hammers or plumbing, but she certainly knew her way around painting.

Then her father sent her a text message needing help with something. Then there was an urgent email from the crematorium to deal with. One task rolled into another until time became a blur.

And she forgot to send Callan a text message about her mother. By the time she remembered, Amanda was on the sidewalk waiting for her, so she didn't bother.

Callan looked surprised to answer his door and find Amanda Cyrs on his doorstep, holding a very large basket full of what was possibly every paint chip ever made. He fixed a smile on his face. Molly saw the warmth spread to his eyes when he saw her.

"Come on in," he said, stepping aside. "Thanks for coming over."

"I meant to text you and tell you Mom was bringing her paint chip collection over, but…" She waved a hand. "There was stuff."

He gave them a quick tour, and it was immediately obvious he was better at the deconstruction than the reconstruction. If she had to bet, she'd say it wouldn't be long before he gave up and called in professional help.

His bedroom was the only room he hadn't started a project in, and it was pretty obvious he was basically living in the room. The wallpaper was ugly and the carpet was probably older than her, but the bed looked new and she tried not to stare at it while he talked about his vision for the place.

She had to admit he'd done a nice job of getting the living room walls ready for painting, but she was pretty sure even she could do that. Changing the wiring in the kitchen or the plumbing in the bathroom? She couldn't do that, and she suspected Callan couldn't, either.

Then again, there was a YouTube video for everything these days.

"You'll definitely want something light and warm in here," Amanda said, turning in circles in the living room.

There was nothing for Molly to do then but watch as her mother held chip after chip against the wall, while Callan nodded or shook his head. A couple of times he scrunched his nose up and Molly giggled.

He kept looking at her and finally he turned to face her. "What do you think, Molly? Any opinions?"

Amanda snorted, but Molly ignored her and pointed at one of the dozen or so chips he had in his hand. "I like that one. The light gray with the hint of…something. Almost a sage green tint. It's very light and warm, but it's kind of elegant and a lot more interesting than white or beige."

His grin warmed away the chill her mother's derision had set on her. "I like it, too. I think this is the winner."

"Perfect." Amanda gathered the chips except that one and dropped them into the basket. "We'll come over Saturday and help you paint. It's an off weekend, right?"

The library was open half days two Saturdays per month, with the librarian having some discretion as to which Saturdays. But Molly wasn't sure her mother should just assume he'd want their help. Or that he didn't have other plans for Saturday.

"I'd really appreciate the help," he said, sounding genuinely grateful and not just polite.

"Excellent. We'll see you Saturday, then. And if anything changes with our schedule, we'll let you know." Then she picked up the basket of paint chips. "Okay, Molly. Let's get out of Callan's way. He's got lots of work to do. And Callan, make sure you stop at the hardware store first thing tomorrow. Jerry opens before the library, so it shouldn't be a problem. But sometimes it takes him a couple of days to get the paint in."

Molly wanted to protest—she would have liked to stay at Callan's a little bit longer—but Amanda was practically pushing her out the door and she didn't want to make a scene.

"I'll see you Saturday, Amanda," he said, and she could tell he was trying not to laugh. "Molly, I'll see you tomorrow between the hardware store and the library."

And that would have to do because her mother was talking to her as she walked back toward their house and she didn't have time to do more than wave to Callan.

But she noticed he kept the door open, leaning against the doorjamb, and watched her until she turned the corner around the fence.

Callan was exhausted by the time Amanda declared the walls were done. Not so much physically, but mentally. The dynamic between mother and daughter was fascinating for him to watch, but it tired him out, too.

They were obviously close and there was a lot of love between them, but Amanda was quick to criticize Molly. And Molly's sense of humor seemed to fade away in the presence of her mother. She seemed hypersensitive to her mother's comments and it bothered him to watch her shoulders sag and the spark leave her eyes.

One thing he wasn't going to do was step into a situation that he knew nothing about and that was none of his business, but he made sure to smile at Molly whenever he could. And she noticed. It perked her up a little each time.

"Done just in time," Amanda said as she pounded the lid back onto a paint can. "It's about time for me to start the meat loaf. Will be you joining us, Callan?"

He loved meat loaf and hadn't had it homemade in a long time, but he also thought maybe Molly had had enough mother-daughter time today. And he hadn't had enough Callan-Molly time.

"I appreciate the invitation, but I already texted a pizza order for delivery for Molly and me because she's going to help me put together a bookshelf." The lie rolled off his tongue, but the way Molly smiled at him made it worth it. "I hope that doesn't mess up your dinner plans."

Amanda waved away his concerns. "Paul loves leftover meat loaf sandwiches, so don't even worry about it."

"Meat loaf takes a while, so we'll clean up," Molly said, and Callan was annoyed that Amanda managed to give her explicit instructions for cleaning the brushes and rollers three times before she got out the door.

He could hear Molly's sigh of relief from all the way across the living room. "I appreciate your help today. With the three of us, it went so fast."

Molly smiled. "My mom definitely knows how to paint walls."

He went to the fridge and poured them each a drink—a soda for him and a water for her. The house didn't have central air-conditioning and it was already starting to get too warm for comfort. He might be able to get by with box fans in the windows for a while, but he'd need a window unit in his bedroom at least pretty soon.

After a few minutes of companionable silence, he cleared his throat. It was time to lighten the mood. "I heard an interesting rumor today."

"That's a good thing," she said, turning her head to smile at him. "Being in on the rumors means people are getting comfortable with you."

"I'm not sure overhearing something, not that I was deliberately eavesdropping, counts as being in on the rumor. Which was about you, by the way."

Her smile immediately turned into a scowl of confusion. "About us, you mean?"

"No, just you." He gave her a mock stern look. "There's a rumor going around Stonefield that you waged a campaign to stuff the Books & Brews ballot box."

Even in the dim lighting he could see the guilty flush coloring her cheeks a rosy pink. "I think 'waged a campaign' is a little strong. I just told people which book I thought would be the most fun to read."

"How many people?"

"Anybody who stood still for more than thirty seconds, I guess." She gave him a playful smile that turned him inside out. "Okay, maybe it was a little bit of a campaign. But you were being very stubborn."

"I don't think picking a book that's been made into a movie is a good idea."

"Why not?"

He thought it was obvious, but maybe not. "Because people will just watch the movie instead of reading the book."

"So? I think finding and comparing all the differences between the book and the movie would make for a lively discussion."

"But it's a book club."

"I swear, Callan, if you were wearing a tie right now, I'd wonder if the knot was too tight. Sometimes it's okay to color outside the lines, you know."

He was about to tell her that the lines were there for a very good reason, but he stopped himself before the words left his lips. Molly knew the lines were there for a reason. And he knew that she had to work harder than other people to stay inside those lines. Maybe instead of trying to keep her coloring neat, he could try coloring messy. Not too much because it simply wasn't in his nature, but he was willing to compromise.

"Maybe you're right," he said, and the way her face lit up was all the reward he could hope for. "Comparing the differences would be fun, and maybe some of the people who watched the movie will be intrigued enough to read more books that have been adapted."

"Trust me. It's going to be *so* fun. Unless somebody gets too into the brews part of Books & Brews and takes exception to somebody's opinion of the book." When he groaned, she laughed and put her hand on his arm. "I'm kidding. That definitely won't happen. Probably."

At this very second Callan didn't care if a drunken fight about the book broke every glass in the taproom. All he cared about was the feel of Molly's hand on his arm. She touched him a lot, and he was surprised by how much he liked it. He hadn't had a lot of touchy-feely people in his life after his mother died, though Mrs. Grant had always given him a fierce hug whenever he went back to visit. Even the women he'd dated had been more reserved and quiet, like he was.

But he really liked it, he thought.

"We should clean up before the paint totally dries," he said, knowing the spell would be broken when she moved away from him. "But first I need to order a pizza because I didn't actually do that."

She dropped her hand and stepped away, just as he'd planned. "What about the bookshelf? If I'm putting together furniture, I think cheesy fries would be a nice bonus."

He laughed. "No bookshelf *yet*, but I'll throw in cheesy fries as a down payment on your future help."

It took longer than expected to thoroughly clean the brushes and rollers so they could be used again, but that gave Callan plenty of time to give himself a stern talking-to.

When it came to fake dating Molly, Callan needed to keep his crayon inside the lines.

Chapter Nine

*Callan Avery will be hosting an open house
on Tuesday evening with extended hours for
anybody who is interested in learning how
you can get ebooks and audiobooks through
the library for free! Whether you already use
an ebook reader or you want to learn more
about them, the library is here to serve you,
and if you stop by the library between 4:00 and
7:00 p.m., Mr. Avery will help you out!*
— Stonefield Gazette *Facebook Page*

Molly tapped her pen on the pad of sticky notes,
trying to decide which three things from her notebook she had to accomplish today. Nothing particularly urgent jumped out at her, which meant sifting

through pages of things she had to do when she got a chance.

Today, she had a chance. Nothing urgent required her attention. Everything was under control as far as the funeral home went, other than needing to flip through some of the industry publications her father subscribed to in order to keep on top of any conventions or continuing education events he might want to attend.

Her mind didn't want to focus on things to do, though. Her brain was definitely more focused on a *person* to do.

Callan Avery was the only thing she wanted to think about at any given time, and it was becoming a problem. They'd been fake dating for three weeks now and she supposed their pretense was probably a success. They were seen in public because they'd meet at the café, she popped into the library frequently and he'd hang out at the taproom when she was there. The community was coming to like him. Neither of them had been caught making out with anybody else.

They were great at fake dating.

So great at it, as a matter of fact, that Molly was starting to feel as if she really had a boyfriend. But he was a boyfriend who didn't kiss her. Or try to sneak second base. Or third. She'd never been able to figure out exactly which body parts corresponded with which stolen bases, but she knew she was in the mood for Callan to hit a home run.

None of that could be written on her sticky note, of course. One, because she only put things on her to-do sticky that were in her sole power to complete. Maybe *send Callan stronger signals* was an action task, but she wasn't sure how to do that.

And two, sometimes sticky notes came unstuck from notebooks and stuck on pants or handbags, only to fall off in the street or her parents' kitchen. She might want Stonefield talking about her and Callan as a couple, but she didn't need *invite Callan to round my bases* to be conversation around the town's dinner tables.

With a growl of frustration—mostly sexual frustration with a side of being annoyed with herself—Molly tossed the sticky note pad back in the basket and closed her notebook. It was going to be a low executive function day after a restless night, and she gave herself permission to just roll with it today.

Her first stop was the Perkin' Up Café because Chelsea was one of her favorite people when she wasn't punishing her with plain decaf coffee. She was almost to the door, thinking about what she wanted to order, when she came to an abrupt stop.

Something was happening in the storefront next to Chelsea's, which had recently been emptied. It had been an insurance office until it closed down because the husband and wife who'd run it wanted to retire and, since most people handled things like that online these days, they didn't bother trying to sell it.

But now the huge windows on either side of the door were covered with newspaper, all hodgepodge with what looked like hundreds of pieces of masking tape. Somebody *really* didn't want anybody peeking inside.

Molly loved a mystery.

Unfortunately this was a mystery that wasn't offering her any clues. Maybe if she walked by at night and the lights were on inside, she'd be able to see shadows through the newsprint, but for now there was nothing to do but keep walking.

She'd spent long enough being frustrated by her to-do list situation that she'd missed the morning rush. That meant she'd missed Callan, which wasn't awesome, but it also meant Chelsea was the only person in the café.

"What's with the newspaper in the windows next door?" she asked after ordering a creamy caramel mocha.

Chelsea shrugged. "I don't know. Whoever did it must have done it overnight, though. It wasn't there when I drove by last night, but it was all done when I came in to open."

Since the Perkin' Up Café opened at dark o'clock, Molly shuddered. She was *so* not a morning person, though she kept trying to force herself to be, since it seemed like everybody in her life went to bed by eleven and was up with the sun. Left to her own devices, she'd rather be up until two in the morning, and then sleep until nine or ten. Her parents had never been on board with that plan, though, and they were not only her parents but her employers and her landlords. She could only push things so far because unofficially working at the taproom when she was in the mood wasn't going to pay rent if they got fed up and threw her out.

"I haven't heard about anybody in Stonefield starting a business, though. What do you think's going in there?" she asked, her mind starting to cough up possibilities.

"I don't know, but I hope it's a business that attracts a lot of caffeine-starved foot traffic."

Maybe it's a sex shop."

Chelsea snorted. "In this town? Unlikely."

"Maybe that's why there's newspaper on the windows."

"I doubt the newspaper's permanent. And do you really think a town that's forcing a single librarian to have a fake girlfriend in order to keep his job is going to allow a sex shop right on the main street?"

"Good point. Although, some of the people on the zoning board are also on the library committee, so they might have tried to sneak it by. Or maybe it's a tattoo parlor."

"I can't decide if that's more or *less* likely than a sex shop."

"Stonefield needs some shaking up."

"Let them get fully accustomed to having a librarian who has a penis before you ask them to let somebody sell fake ones."

Molly laughed. "You know what we need in this town? A psychic. Or a stationery store. Or maybe somebody who's really good at nail art."

"If Stonefield ever gets a strip mall, I hope they let you pick all the stores."

"Maybe I should run for a seat on the planning committee."

Chelsea arched her eyebrow. "That sounds fun. Monthly meetings. Agendas. Paperwork."

"Or maybe not. I'm bored today, but not *that* bored."

"Speaking of things you get up to when you're bored, how are things going with your fake boyfriend?"

Molly wrinkled her nose. She didn't want to tell her friends how things were going—that the fake part was going so swell, she wanted it to be real. Their total lack of surprise that one of her impromptu plans had gone awry again would be annoying.

"Good," she said.

A group of women entered, probably moms who'd dropped their kids off at school, which put an end to talking about Callan. A half hour later, still bored and now hopped up on caffeine and sugar, Molly left to find something else to do.

She ended up spending most of the day at Evie's house, playing with the baby while they brainstormed content for the brewery's social media accounts. Becca was just shy of four months old now, and Molly was amazed by how fast babies changed, even if it had only been days since she'd seen her.

Now that Mallory's boys were older, she was glad there was a new round of babies because she adored them. She'd never have her own because she wouldn't wish her brain chemistry on anyone, but she loved the Sutton kids like a real auntie.

Despite the distraction of the cutest baby girl ever born, they managed to come up with a list of photo ideas to stage in the taproom, as well as a few event ideas to run by the rest of the family.

Molly was on her way home from Sutton's Seconds, where she'd been hoping to score some cute summer tops before it got hot and everybody wanted one, when she passed the library. She'd never seen the parking lot so full, and it took her a moment to remember Callan was hosting an open house about digital reading tonight.

He could probably use some help. And by Stonefield standards, Molly would probably be considered an early adopter, and she knew quite a bit about ebooks. She could help, plus there were a *lot* of people in the library, so it was a perfect opportunity to show off what a devoted girlfriend Callan had.

The relief in his eyes when he saw her was so obvious, she had to laugh. He clearly hadn't expected this kind of turnout, and he'd made some impressively informative poster board displays, but the patrons were looking for one-on-one help. She set her bags behind the circulation desk, since being the librarian's girlfriend probably came with permission to be back there, and asked the closest patron how she could help.

"My daughter bought me this phone the last time she came to visit," Mrs. Brown told her. "She put this app on it so I can listen to my murder mysteries while I knit, and I can figure out how to stop and start it, but I don't know how to put another book on it. I've listened to the murder mysteries she put on it five times and no matter how much wine I have with my dinner, I still remember whodunnit."

"I'm familiar with that app, so I can help you."

"I have my password written down in my purse, but you better not tell anybody what it is."

"I would never, Mrs. Brown."

As she passed behind Mrs. Brown, Molly gave Callan a smile, which he returned. They made a good team, she thought, and judging by the comments she overheard over the course of the open house, she wasn't alone. Everybody was buying their relationship status, and his popularity with library patrons was definitely on the rise. It wouldn't be long before a voice against him based on ignorance would be drowned out by his supporters.

She'd have mixed feelings when that day came. It would mean her impulsive plan had been successful, which rarely happened. She wouldn't mind the win. On the other hand, it would also mean Callan didn't need a fake girlfriend anymore. But she didn't need to worry about that right now, since she had him at least until Gwen's wedding since he had to be her plus-one. She had another two and a half weeks.

When the last patron was gone, Callan leaned against the circulation desk and his body sagged slightly as he exhaled slowly. "I didn't expect that many people to show up. If you hadn't jumped in, I would have been here until midnight."

"I think that's the most people I've ever seen in the library at one time, so congratulations, Mr. Avery."

"Thank you. I got to renew some expired cards for people who didn't realize they could still use the library even if they wanted to read ebooks. And I issued some new ones, so I think it was a raging success. I should buy you dinner to thank you for your help."

Molly was pretty sure her entire body flushed with heat, and she really hoped it didn't show in her face. "The diner makes great burgers. Their fries are good, too."

He smiled, his eyes warm. "I could go for a burger."

They walked hand in hand from the library to the diner. It just kind of happened. He'd locked up and they started walking. Their hands brushed and then their fingers were interlocked. Apparently, deception came easier to him than he'd expected because nothing felt more natural to him than holding Molly's hand.

Lately he'd been wondering during what kind of public situations a man might be expected to kiss his girlfriend. If he could figure that out, he might actually find a way to kiss her. Finally.

It couldn't be the library. That was his place of work and it just wouldn't sit right. And the taproom was out because most of the people who'd be paying attention there knew they weren't a real couple.

Walking her home and kissing her good-night was a possibility. It was a residential neighborhood and anybody sitting on their front porch or glancing out a window would probably think it odd if he *didn't* kiss her. But he wasn't sure he wanted to kiss Molly for the first time with one or both of her parents watching from behind a curtain. It had been hard enough keeping up the pretense through the four family dinners he'd been invited to so far. He didn't want to make it worse by adding kissing into the mix. The more they believed he was the one their daughter had a future with, the worse he was going to feel facing them when he and Molly ended their relationship.

There were still two and a half weeks until Gwen and Case's wedding, but he knew they'd have to have a conversation about how and when to end things eventually. But probably not before he kissed her.

Maybe when they parted ways after a morning meetup at the Perkin' Up Café. There were always enough people around to merit a performance. And a *have a good day, honey* kiss would be perfectly normal.

"You're quiet tonight," Molly said, squeezing her hand. "What are you thinking about?"

He wasn't going to risk ruining their dinner—it might technically be their first date outside of the taproom—by confessing he was trying to find a within-the-rules way of kissing his fake girlfriend.

"Just tired, I guess. I stay up on all the latest technology and advances in accessibility, but actually walking patrons through the steps was a lot more exhausting than I thought it would be."

She was laughing when he had to let go of her hand to pull open the door to the diner. "If it makes you feel any better, I don't think anybody could tell."

The diner wasn't very busy since this wasn't the big city and most people had already eaten. Plus, it was a weeknight. As far as he could tell, the diner made most of their money on Friday nights with the all-you-can-eat fish fry and with Sunday-morning breakfast.

Molly led him to a booth that was in view of everybody, but far enough from the few other diners so they'd be able to talk privately if they kept their voices down.

"I guess it's too late for coffee," she said as she slid onto the seat. "And I can see what's left of the decaf from here and it looks like that pot's been sitting awhile. I guess I'll have to have water, which is so boring."

"There's always soda. They have some that are caffeine-free."

"The sugar, though." She laughed. "I never drink soda because the sugar wreaks havoc on my brain. If I had one right now, I'd be going door-to-door at 2:00 a.m., looking for somebody to go on adventures with me."

He wouldn't mind her knocking on his door at two in the morning looking for an adventure, but he kept that to himself. And when the server arrived, he ordered an ice water for each of them. They both asked for burgers and fries without even looking at the menus.

"Just so you know," Molly said when they were alone again, "if you start rewarding me coming to the library with cheeseburgers, you'll never get rid of me."

"A cheeseburger is a small price to pay for you helping out me out. You're doing a lot of work just to get a plus-one for a friend's wedding."

"Sometimes it's nice to not be the third wheel. Or the seventh wheel, as the case may be. And you'll look really good standing next to me in the reception photos."

"I'll try not to look like a startled deer."

"Evie had run off to Arizona because she and Lane broke up—again—and she didn't know she was pregnant, so she attended Mallory's wedding by video chat. Maybe Rome can be there virtually and distract you every time somebody's going to take a picture."

"I bet it would amuse the hell out of him to get an invitation to virtually attend his best friend's fake girlfriend's best friend's older sister's wedding."

She laughed. "That's quite a mouthful."

"I'm surprised you don't have guys lined up for the chance to be your plus-one, though."

The amusement was gone from her expression in the blink of an eye, replaced by what looked like sadness and frustration. "I don't have a lot of luck dating, actually."

Callan found that hard to believe. Molly was gorgeous and smart and funny, and if she was *really* his, he would fight any man who tried to take her from him. He'd probably lose because he'd never actually been in a fight, but he'd put in one hell of an effort.

Molly laughed. "You should see your face right now. It's pretty flattering, to be honest."

"Maybe there's something in the water, because there is something seriously wrong with the men in this town." He chuckled. "Not that I'm complaining,

of course. Our situation would be a lot more complicated if some other guy had been smart enough to
be your date to the wedding."

"It's not really their fault, though. Guys have tried,
but I'm a lot and it's always just a matter of time before I go from *a lot* to *too much*." She said the words
flippantly enough, but Callan could hear the pain in
her voice, and he could see it in her eyes.

"I'm glad you don't make yourself smaller to fit
into anybody else's idea of what you should be," he
said, and her cheeks flushed. Her eyes also looked
a little damp, though, and he didn't want her to cry
so it was time to bring the conversation back to light
and easy. "And not just because I would have missed
out on a free dinner at Case and Gwen's wedding."

Amusement chased the shadows from her eyes.
"And cake! Mallory went to the cake tasting with
Gwen and she said if we fill up on wedding chicken
before the cake is cut, we'll be very, very sorry."

"Is it carrot cake?" He was pretty sure that was a
popular wedding cake in New England, but he wasn't
sure.

Her nose wrinkled. "I hope not. Mal wouldn't tell
me because Gwen wants it to be a surprise, but I am
very opposed to vegetables in my desserts."

"Same," he said, and she clinked her water glass
against his before taking a sip.

Molly continued talking about the wedding—
apparently finding the perfect dress for the preg-

nant and picky matron of honor had been quite an ordeal—and Callan was content to sit back and listen. Wedding details weren't something he'd ordinarily be interested in, but he loved watching Molly talk about things that excited her.

Her hands were almost as animated as her facial expressions and he feared for her water glass a few times. She felt things on a magnified scale, he'd noticed. She didn't just like something. It was the *best thing ever*. On the flip side, things that others might shrug off as inconsequential cut her deeply. For Callan, who'd gone through life on a fairly even keel—except for the dark times surrounding losing his mother—it was definitely a different energy.

Just a matter of time before I go from a lot *to* too much.

"So that's why you can't wear bright or primary colors to the wedding."

He realized he'd missed something, but he didn't want her thinking he was uninterested. The problem had been the exact opposite. "Is there a particular color you'd like for me to wear?"

She thought about it for a few seconds, tilting her head. "What color is your suit?"

"I have several. Black, dark gray, and navy."

"The navy one, but the tie will be harder. You might have to send me pictures of your ties so I can look at them with my dress."

"I'll do that."

"Okay, enough wedding talk," she said with a wave of her hand. "How is the remodeling going?"

"Slowly," he admitted. "I'm trying not to make too much of a mess in multiple parts of the house at the same time, but it's an old structure and one thing to work on keeps leading to two more things that need to be done to finish it."

They talked about the renovation as they finished their dinner, and he promised to consider her notebook and sticky note method of prioritizing things around the house. He paid the bill and he unconsciously rested his hand at the small of Molly's back as they walked through the diner.

There was a family eating ice cream in a booth near the door, and Callan recognized the man as one who'd been very unhappy to realize the man behind the circulation desk was the new librarian. His gaze bounced between Molly and Callan. Then the man gave him a friendly nod and went back to ice cream.

Callan tamped down the annoyance. That the man's acceptance of him in a professional capacity had been changed by being in a relationship with Molly was still one of the most ludicrous things he'd ever encountered. But he was having a nice time, so he chose to focus on the fact the ruse appeared to be working.

They held hands on the walk home, and Callan could feel his anxiety rising as they reached the corner of their street. He wasn't going to know a second's peace until he'd kissed this woman, and he couldn't face another sleepless night. He'd actually gotten the alphabet wrong while shelving fiction returns today.

When they reached the spot where they'd go separate directions—her up the drive to the garage and him past the fence to his walkway—he squeezed her hand and she looked up at him.

"I should walk you to your door," he said. "We wouldn't want the neighborhood to think I'm a bad boyfriend."

"We definitely don't want that."

But when they reached the access door to the side of the big overhead doors, he didn't let go of her hand. Even though they'd established people might be watching and they should act like a real couple, he wasn't sure how to transition to kissing her. Maybe she didn't want to take the ruse that far and he didn't want to overstep, or put her in the awkward position of not knowing how to say no.

Then she gave him a naughty-looking smile and stepped closer, tilting her head back. "I would never be in a relationship with a guy who doesn't want to kiss me good-night after a date."

That was all the invitation Callan needed. His mouth claimed hers with such intensity, nobody who happened to see it would doubt that he was *very* into Molly. As his tongue dipped between her lips, he worried it was too much, but she had her arms around his neck and she wasn't letting go.

Then she made the sweetest moaning sound against his mouth and Callan knew he had to stop. He didn't *want* to, but after a few more delicious seconds, he broke the kiss off and put some space between their bodies. She looked as flushed as he felt as her arms fell to her side and their gazes locked.

If this was real, she'd probably take his hand and lead him up those stairs. Or they'd pass by the fence and head for *his* bed. But it wasn't, and the performance was over for now.

"Good night, Molly."

"Good night." Her smile was tinged with sadness and for a few seconds he thought maybe they *could* go up those stairs. This chemistry between them wasn't fake at all. "Thank you for dinner."

There was nothing else he could say because, like it or not—and he did not like it—she'd offered to pretend to be his girlfriend and nothing more. And he couldn't be sure his own need wasn't making him misread her signals. So he nodded and then, with a heaviness settling in his chest, turned and walked back to the sidewalk to continue past the fence and up his walk. Alone.

Chapter Ten

The Stonefield Fire Department would like to remind everybody that permits are required for all burning on your property, including camp-fire rings. And using Photoshop to change the dates on last year's permits won't work because they keep records. The chief's official comment was "we weren't born last night." You can find their office hours on the town's website.
—Stonefield Gazette *Facebook Page*

"So what is Old Home Day all about, anyway?"

Molly laughed, until she realized Callan was seri-ous. They were sitting in the café, though not at her favorite table because Daphne and a prospective cli-ent had beat them there. They'd even met up in front of her house earlier than usual so they could take their time having coffee together before he opened the library and she went with her father to clean several of the old granite headstones in the cemetery.

It was one of the many side hustles her parents engaged in because not enough people died in Stonefield and the surrounding towns each year to support the funeral home. That was good, of course, but it also meant jobs on the side. Amanda wrote articles for trade publications and when things were particularly slow, she sometimes picked up serving hours at a fancy restaurant her friend owned in the city.

"I'm serious," Callan insisted. "I think Mrs. Denning spent more time lecturing me about Old Home Day than she did anything else."

"It's very important."

"It's a used book sale."

She shook her head. "It's not only a library fundraiser. Old Home Day is when we get a parade and kettle corn and we get to buy lots of used books. A lot of people look forward to the sale all year."

"I do like kettle corn."

"Who doesn't?" Molly took a sip of her coffee. "I guess like over a hundred years ago or whatever, young people were moving away from small towns looking for work or fun and stuff. So somebody who was presumably in charge of something made a holiday that was to encourage the people who moved away to return to their hometowns for a day of celebration."

"There's a lot of missing information in that sentence, but I get the gist. Do a lot of people who've moved away from Stonefield come back for the day?"

She laughed. "Not really. The ones who do come back to visit usually do the Fourth of July or Labor Day so they have a long weekend."

"It'll be a workday for me, I guess. I haven't really had time to find a high schooler willing to volunteer as a page until I can push a wage for them through the budget committee."

"Yeah, Mrs. Denning had trouble keeping volunteers. Maybe because she didn't really like teenagers. Or kids. Or most adults, really. We'll be able to watch the parade together, though."

As soon as she said the words, she realized making plans for them as a couple that far out probably wasn't a good idea. But Old Home Day was only a couple of weeks after Gwen's wedding. Even if they'd done the breaking up part of the deal by then, they could still watch a parade together. They'd probably still be friends.

"I brought your coffee to go," Chelsea said, appearing at Molly's side with a very large to-go cup for Callan. "I put it on your tab."

"You get a tab?" Molly asked. "Chelsea, you barely even know him!"

"Hey!" Callan protested with mock outrage.

"Oh, so you can *date* him, but I can't extend him credit?" Chelsea said.

"I'm your friend and I don't have a tab," Molly pointed out.

"You have very expensive taste in caffeine. Callan doesn't and rather than go through the system for each small transaction, it's easier to run it once a week."

Once Chelsea walked away, Molly gave Callan the sternest look she could muster. "You're not allowed to have that in the library."

His laughter turned heads, and she couldn't help but laugh with him. She still couldn't believe she thought he didn't have a sense of humor when they first met. He did, and it complemented hers rather nicely.

"I don't take my coffee around the books," he said. "It stays in my office."

"So I can bring my drink in and put it in your office and then when I'm looking at books, I can just pop in every time I want a sip."

"You're not authorized personnel. Sorry. Do you have time to walk with me to the library?" he asked, and she looked at her phone.

She did, though she couldn't stay very long. Not only did he have work to do, but her dad would be waiting for her. It wasn't as though there was a scheduled time to clean the gravestones, but her dad liked to tackle the big jobs early in the day. And even though they couldn't technically be late if there wasn't an appointment, he'd probably still lecture her on her "utter lack of respect for the concept of time."

"Sure," she said, and the smile he gave her in response was genuine.

As he threw away their garbage and she gave Chelsea a goodbye wave as she served a customer, Molly couldn't help the warmth of pleasure that seeped through her.

The coffee date had been plenty to satisfy the town's curiosity about them. And maybe her walking him to work would add a little extra oomph, but she could tell by the way he'd looked at her that there was more to it than that.

Callan Avery actually enjoyed her company.

He let them in the back door of the library, mostly because the lockset was newer and the keys for the front doors tended to stick. After flipping on just the light over the circulation desk, he prepared himself to broach the topic he'd been thinking about a lot lately.

How to end their relationship.

But Molly had already wandered off and was looking around the stacks. "There seem to be a lot of empty spaces on the shelves. Did Mrs. Denning not tell you that when people return their books, you're supposed to reshelve them?"

He chuckled, the cheeky look she gave him taking any insult out of her words. "I've started weeding the collection, so I think it's going to be a banner used book sale this year."

"You might need more quilts."

He sighed, remembering how insistent Mrs. Denning was that the residents of Stonefield expected the used books to be displayed face-up on quilts across the library lawn. It made for an inviting display, and nobody liked to look at the spines in boxes. It was the covers that drew people in. Since he was new, he was going to try it her way this year rather than inflict too many changes on the town, but if he came up with a better way, he'd try that next year.

Assuming this charade didn't blow up in his face and drive him out of town on a wave of humiliation, of course.

"She wasn't really clear on what to do with books left over, though," he said. "Will recycling take them?"

"Throwing away books is very sad, Callan." She wandered back to the circulation desk, where he was sorting through the notes he'd left himself before locking up last night.

"Nobody hates it more than I do, Molly, but if a book is so past its prime it's weeded out of a library's collection and then it goes unwanted at a fundraising used book sale, it's time for it to be recycled into paper or to-go coffee cups or something."

Her eyes lit up at the mention of coffee. "Oh, now I'll be wondering if my coffee cups used to be books.

Maybe a passionate romance novel or a science fiction adventure."

"Or a book on how to invest in the stock market from 1986," he said, and she groaned. "You don't find many unwanted romance novels."

"Yes, but—oh!" She slapped his arm. "Didn't Mrs. Denning tell you about Flea Market Guy?"

"Um, no? I assume that's his job and not his name, though."

"I can never remember his name. Anyway, Flea Market Guy will probably show up right before the book sale ends and he'll give you a lowball offer for whatever books are left."

"And did Mrs. Denning usually accept Flea Market Guy's lowball offer?"

"Of course. What else would she do with the books? And a few dollars is better than no dollars."

"That solves that problem," he said. "But I don't—"

"Wait. I almost forgot. Make sure you keep your eye on Flea Market Guy when he's loading up the books, though. Mrs. Denning caught him with one of the quilts once and he said it was an accident, but those are a lot more valuable than a 1986 stock market guide in a flea market." She grinned. "Unless you're a time traveler. Maybe if you could go back in time, you'd want to invest in some of the super-valuable companies from our time, but if you're from now, you might not know how the stock market worked back then. You could read that book and go back in time and then become like a mega-bil-lionaire."

He really loved the way her mind worked. "Maybe I should set it aside, then."

"You should see if there's a book on how to build a time machine and bundle them together for a big price."

"Or take them home and learn how to become a mega-billionaire myself," he pointed out and he was rewarded with one of her joyful laughs.

"I'd tell you take me with you, but I'd probably get distracted and hit the dials and we'd end up in 1886 instead and I'd have to wear a corset."

"Worth it to be rich, though, right?"

She thought about it for a few seconds. "I think if you tried to invest in Apple in 1886, you'd just end up with an orchard."

"Good point." He shook his head, finding it hard to believe he was enjoying talking about investments and time travel. "On a more serious note, I have to unlock the doors in a few minutes, but I've been thinking about this arrangement of ours."

He was surprised when she scowled and crossed her arms in front of her chest. "I hope you don't think a few trips to the Perkin' Up Café and cheeseburgers at the diner will be enough. You're supposed to be my plus-one at Gwen and Case's wedding, remember?"

Her temper rose almost as quickly as her excite-ment levels, but strangely, she was quieter when she was mad than when she was happy. She had a *very* expressive face, though. "Of course I remember. I wasn't talking about ending it right now."

"Oh." Her arms fell to her sides and her face brightened. "So what about it?"

"We should have an *idea* of when we're going to have our breakup. Just so we're on the same page and all that." And having a calendar date to keep his eye on would help keep him focused on the pretense and not on his relationship with Molly. He hoped.

"Not really a go-with-the-flow kind of guy, huh?" she teased.

"No, I'm very much *not* that guy."

"Okay, so after Gwen's wedding."

"But not right after," he said. "Weddings are pretty joyous occasions, so we should let that ride for a while. Like, at least a week."

"A whole week of joy?" She laughed. "Okay, but breaking up a week after Gwen's wedding means a week before Old Home Day. And if we break up then, everybody will be talking about it."

He frowned, resisting the urge to pull up the town's website and check their calendar of events alongside his own, the library's and the Sutton family's. There was a possibility if he had to work around all of those schedules, he'd end up spending the rest of his life with this woman. That was *not* the plan, though he was starting to think maybe that wouldn't be so bad.

"I think after Old Home Day is best," she said in

an uncharacteristically quiet voice. "There's no week of joy after that. Everybody just goes back to their lives, so it'll just be the regular amount of gossip.

That meant he'd be fake dating Molly for almost two months before they were done. It was a long time to build a relationship, pretend or not, and considering they weren't even halfway through it, he knew it was going to be hard to call it quits. They'd be good friends with established habits by then, if nothing else.

It was the *nothing else* that worried him, which is why he'd wanted to set an expiration date. He might even circle it in red on his calendars so he'd have something tangible to look at if the line between pretend and reality started blurring on him again.

His phone's alarm sent the sound of a doorbell through the library and he sighed. "Time for me to open."

"I'll unlock the doors on my way out," Molly said. "But before I go, Mom asked me to invite you over for herbed chicken tonight."

"I do like herbed chicken." It was a sweet bonus to their arrangement. "Are you sure it's not imposing?"

"Of course not. They love having company. And I warned you they'd invite you over a lot."

"It'll make it easier to renovate my kitchen," he pointed out, and she laughed.

"I'll see you tonight," she called as she undid the bolts on the old wooden doors and stepped out into the sunshine.

Chapter Eleven

*A quick reminder that Sutton's Place Brewery
& Tavern, Sutton's Seconds, and D&T Tree
Service are taking a four-day weekend to celebrate a family wedding. They'll close at their
regular times Thursday and reopen Tuesday
morning. While they don't foresee any beer
or thrifting emergencies, if you have a tree-
related emergency, D&T's outgoing greeting
will provide information on how to get help
while they're away.*

—Stonefield Gazette *Facebook Page*

"This is gorgeous, Gwen," Molly said, spinning in
a slow circle to take everything in.

The historic lakefront inn an hour north of Stonefield was a perfect wedding venue. Besides the stately white bed-and-breakfast and the water, there were flowers and lawns and arches and she knew the photographer was going to be ecstatic.

"We ran a little late," Gwen said about their convoy of cars. "So once we get all the bags to our rooms, we'll have to head straight out to the table. No messing around."

When Gwen said there was no messing around, nobody messed around. They put their luggage on carts and took turns waiting for the two elevators. Her room was simple, but pretty and bright, and she wanted to flop onto the bed and enjoy it, but she couldn't be late to Gwen's bachelorette party.

A lot of ideas had been floated for the party, with everything from strippers to a weekend in Vegas on the table. Stonefield didn't have strippers and none of them could really afford to fly to Las Vegas for a weekend, so they'd stopped trying to make it spectacular and gone instead for an evening that would make Gwen happy.

Under a canopy lit by fairy lights and electric candles was a long table where Gwen and the women she loved were going to have a five-course dinner served to them. None of them had to cook or clear the table or wash the dishes. There was no loud music to shout over or games to play. Gwen just wanted to spend the evening before she got married enjoying the company of her mother and sisters, Laura, and Molly, who was kind of a fake sister.

She did the fake thing pretty well, Molly thought.

"Have I thanked you ever so much for getting married while I'm so very pregnant?" Mallory asked Gwen once the dinner plates had been cleared and they were waiting a few minutes before having dessert brought out. There had been a *lot* of food.

"Only two dozen times," Gwen replied. "So for the twenty-fifth time, they had two openings, and it was either a very pregnant matron of honor or a newly postpartum matron of honor juggling my bouquet and a screaming newborn."

"Yeah, pregnant's better," Mallory admitted while the rest of them laughed because this wasn't the first or even fifth time they'd had this conversation.

"I'm waiting for Irish to call a time-out during the ceremony," Evie said. "So Mallory can sit and put her feet up for a few minutes."

Gwen, who had just taken a sip of her cocktail, almost choked and Ellen gave her a couple of thumps on her back. Molly was happy to see they were unnecessary because the bride leaving in an ambulance would really rain on their bachelorette party parade.

"It's sweet how determined that man is to take care of me and this baby," Mallory said once Gwen stopped coughing. "And I never would have believed I'd say this, but it *is* possible to spend too much time sitting around doing nothing."

"He's such a good man," Ellen said, and Molly could hear the emotion in her voice. She'd been emotional since they arrived, though she'd been able to smile through most of it. "They all are. You girls chose well. And I can't believe tomorrow all three of you will be married."

"What are you going to do about your books?" Molly asked Gwen, impulsively changing the subject to ward off the inevitable tears. And also because she'd been wondering about it all day. "Do they have to change the name on the covers?"

"Nope. If I take Case's last name, my legal name now will become my pseudonym going forward because my career was built as Gwen Sutton. It's not realistic to think readers would see a Gwen Danforth novel and think, 'Hey, I wonder if Gwen Sutton got married and changed her name,' you know?"

"You're getting married *tomorrow* and you don't know if you're taking his last name?" Evie asked. "You've been engaged forever."

"It's complicated, though. I mean, it's not just about my personal identity. It's my professional identity and I don't know if I want those to be two separate things."

Evie nodded. "What does Case think?"

"He's good either way. He gets it. And he said when we have kids, we could hyphenate theirs to Danforth-Sutton, but that's a bit of a mouthful."

"I heard couples are starting to merge their last

names into a whole new name," Molly said. "What would that be? Danton? Sutforth?"

They all laughed as Gwen shook her head so emphatically her plastic tiara slipped. "I'm leaning toward using Danforth personally and Sutton professionally, but I'm not jumping through paperwork hoops until I'm sure."

They brought the desserts out and the women of the wedding party talked about tomorrow's schedule while they all ate decadent desserts none of them had room for. Molly didn't put in the effort of paying attention since none of it was really applicable. She was *like* family and Gwen had wanted her here tonight, but she didn't have any responsibilities when it came to the ceremony and reception. She was free to concentrate on the thickest, creamiest cheesecake she'd ever eaten in her life.

Until she heard her name.

"I can't imagine what you girls' rooms will look like by the time the guys switch tomorrow night," Ellen was saying. "Especially Molly's. Poor Callan will be lucky if he can find a spot for his toothbrush."

Molly had a lifetime of hiding stress responses from people, so she joined in the laughter and nobody seemed to notice she was freaking out on the inside.

The wings of the inn were essentially divided into the bride's squad and the groom's squad for the night since that was how everybody would get ready for the ceremony. But tomorrow night, they'd be rearranged. There were two suites. The honeymoon suite was obviously reserved for Case and Gwen. Laura and Ellen were taking the two-bedroom suite because they'd have Becca, Jack and Eli with them. Irish would move to Mallory's room. Lane would move to Evie's room.

And Callan would move to Molly's room.

She'd known that, of course, but they'd all been so busy preparing for the weekend, she hadn't really given any thought to what it *meant*. And, more importantly, she wasn't sure Callan knew they'd be sharing a room.

It was too late to do anything about it. Even if he was so opposed to sharing a room with her that he wanted to return to Stonefield and sleep in his own bed, he didn't have his car. And she didn't think he'd be *so* against it that he'd pay whatever astronomical cost it would be to Uber back. But she should give him a heads-up and give him the chance to figure out how he felt about it rather than springing it on him when the guys arrived from wherever they'd gone.

Funny story, she typed into their message thread. You know how the men and women are staying in separate wings tonight so the party and pre-wedding stuff can happen? During the wedding, it's all being moved around so the couples are together.

The return text message felt like a long time coming, but finally Callan's words popped up on her screen. Okay. What's the funny part?

Ellen made the reservations and since she's in the dark, she assumed we'd share a room.

I assumed we would, but I can try to find the laughing emoji if you give me a few minutes.

He'd assumed they would be sharing a room? And he hadn't said anything about it? Maybe he didn't quite grasp what she was saying.

There's only one bed.

The dots that indicated he was typing appeared. Then they disappeared and Molly held her breath, but no words appeared before she had to either exhale or pass out. Then the dots appeared again.

We're both adults.

She waited, but there was no follow-up message. What did that mean? They were both adults, so they could sleep in a bed together without it being awkward? Or they were both adults in the consenting sense, and they could share a bed and cross *have hot, sweaty sex with the new librarian* off her sticky note from the morning after they met without it being a big deal? Then her phone chimed again and she almost dropped it in her rush to read his text.

Lane says if I don't put my phone away, he'll take an axe to it.

Molly snorted. They might own a tree service, but Lane doesn't carry axes around with him.

We're at an axe-throwing place.

Her eyes widened. You're throwing axes the night before they take wedding photos?

And they serve alcohol. We're drinking beer and throwing axes.

There was a pause and then, before Molly could respond, another message came through.

Don't tell anybody else.

"Molly, what's going on?" Gwen asked from across the table.

"Nothing." She turned her phone facedown on her lap. "Why? What do you mean?"

"You look like there's something going on, and you literally gasped a few seconds ago."

"Oh." Explaining to Gwen that her groom and his friends were drinking alcohol and throwing axes didn't seem like a good idea, even without Callan asking her not to tell. And of course her brain usually raced around like it was every go-kart on the track at once, but right now it felt as if it had plunged into a mud bog. "Just a text from my mom."

They *all* gasped and Laura covered her mouth with her hand for a few seconds before asking the question Molly might have seen coming if her brain wasn't spinning its wheels. "Oh no. Who died?"

"No!" Outside of family and first responders, her parents were usually the first to know when somebody in Stonefield passed away. "Nobody died, that I know of. It was... She just spoiled a show we watch together. No big deal."

Gwen frowned. "You looked like it was a big deal."

"You know how I am," Molly said breezily with a wave of her hand that almost knocked over her water glass.

They did, in fact, know how she was, so they resumed whatever conversation they'd been having before she attracted Gwen's attention. Once none of them were looking at her, she picked up her phone and sent a quick message to Callan.

None of you better get hurt, but have fun.

They have strict safety protocols. Lane sees me. Gotta go.

If anybody would get annoyed enough to take an axe to somebody's phone, it would be Lane, so Molly didn't bother sending back a farewell text. She set her phone back on the table so her hand was free to pluck a few more of the delectable puff pastries off the stand closest to her.

Chewing food meant she didn't have to be part of the conversation around her, which meant she could worry about the men drinking beer and throwing axes. That was slightly less scary to her than thinking about sharing a room with Callan tomorrow night and what his text message had meant.

We're both adults.

Callan had never been on a party bus before. In his mind, they had neon lights, thumping music, sticky floors and built-in stripper poles. Maybe some did, but the one he'd somehow found himself on was just a bus-shaped version of a limousine, meant to get guests to a destination without anybody having to drive. It seemed overkill for four guys, but Case said it was part of the inn's wedding package and if they were paying for it, they were using it.

It had sat in the parking lot while he and the other guys did the *drink beer and throw axes* thing, which had gone much better than he'd anticipated. The groom and best man had checked off a thing that had apparently been on their bucket list for quite some time, and nobody came out bleeding or missing body parts.

He didn't know Gwen as well as he did Mallory or Evie because she didn't spend a lot of time in the taproom, but he'd heard enough about her to know her wedding photos being ruined by an evening of throwing axes was something they'd all have to hear about for a very long time.

He still wasn't sure why he'd been invited along for Case Danforth's bachelor party. He'd known he'd be Molly's plus-one for the actual wedding, of course, but being told to pack an overnight bag had been a last-minute surprise. It was probably normal if you were dating one of a very tight-knit group of women to be included in their men's plans, but almost everybody involved knew they weren't *really* a couple. Either the suggestion had come from Ellen, or Molly had told them it would look strange to the community—especially Ellen, Laura and her parents—if he didn't go along. And it would, so he'd gone along. There was the cake to look forward to, as well.

And spending the night with Molly in a room with one bed.

He'd been trying not to think too much about that, but it had been on his mind since Irish had casually mentioned the room arrangements, and the fact Ellen had made them. Ellen, who had no idea Callan and Molly were only pretending to be a couple.

Molly hadn't seemed worried about it, though. She hadn't mentioned it and Callan wasn't sure how to bring it up without it sounding like a big deal, so they'd managed to make it all the way to the wedding weekend without having a conversation about sharing a bed.

"Okay, Callan," Lane said, yanking him out of his thoughts. "Be honest. Do you have a book in that duffel bag?"

"Nope." They looked skeptical and he laughed. "You can toss it if you want. There are no books in that bag."

Why would he take up room in his bag with a book when he had hundreds of them on his phone? And usually he'd start tensing up when a group of guys brought up his reading because when he'd been a kid, having his nose in a book often made him a target, but not these guys. They were decent, and since he was the librarian, he knew they were all readers, too. They didn't go through as many books as he did, but they weren't going to ridicule him for reading. This was about something else.

"I was just wondering if you brought along something to keep yourself occupied tomorrow night," Lane continued, and Callan smiled. There it was. "You know about the room arrangements, right?"

"I do." He noticed Case had leaned forward, propping his elbows on his knees, and all three men were looking at him very intensely. He was about to get the *Molly is like a little sister to us* lecture.

"Molly's like a little sister to us," Case said, and it took everything Callan had not to laugh. Even with a couple of beers in him, he knew that would be a mistake. "We know you're supposedly a fake couple—even though it doesn't look like it—but we just…you know."

"Yeah, I know. But Molly's an adult woman, so even if you were *actually* her brothers, it wouldn't really be any of your business who's in her bed." It was a risk to say it, since pissing off three very strong guys who'd been drinking while they were on a back road in the middle of nowhere wasn't a great idea. "I like Molly, though, and I respect her. So what I can tell you is that if we don't make a wall of pillows down the middle of the bed tomorrow night, it will be because *she* chose not to."

"Fair enough," Lane said, and they all relaxed again.

Or *they* did, anyway. Callan found it a little more difficult to put the matter out of his mind because now he not only had to worry about how he and Molly each felt about sharing a room tomorrow night, but that they had an audience on top of it. Not a *literal* audience, of course. But the people in her life were definitely keeping tabs on what was going on between them.

Maybe, if he was lucky, somebody else would figure that out and tell him, because when it came to the status of his fake relationship with Molly, he had no idea what was really going on.

Chapter Twelve

We've heard from many people that the win-
dows of the old Barton Insurance office, next
to the Perkin' Up Café, are covered in news-
paper. We've asked around, but nobody seems
to know what the next new business in Stone-
field will be. We'll be making a lot of trips to
the café for coffee in hopes that Chelsea Grey
will get the scoop on her new neighbor. We'll
let you know if we hear anything, and you do
the same. Our inbox is always open!
　　　　　—Stonefield Gazette *Facebook Page*

Molly didn't get to see Callan until it was almost
time to be seated for the ceremony. Even though
there wasn't really a wedding party—only a matron

of honor and best man—she'd joined Mallory, Evie and Ellen in the bridal suite.

The inn's wedding package included glam for the bride, but Gwen had passed on having her hair and makeup done. Instead, she'd done her own makeup, keeping it subtle, and Ellen had helped her put her hair up. She looked beautiful in a simple white gown, and Mallory looked positively radiant in a sapphire blue dress. Ellen's mother of the bride dress was a lighter shade of the same blue and Molly's eyes teared up as the photographer took photos of them helping Gwen with her veil.

When Ellen pulled a small jewelry box out of her bag, though, Molly quietly slipped out of the room, gesturing for the photographer and wedding planner to follow her. Ellen had shown her the gift several days ago and there had been tears. There were about to be more.

"Give them five minutes," she told them before heading off to find Callan.

In the jewelry box was an exquisite locket with a photo of David Sutton inside. They'd be emotional and missing him badly right now, and even though she was *practically* family, that was a moment for Ellen and her daughters.

She was afraid Callan would be out on the lawn, sitting alone in a chair and waiting for her, but she found him with the guys, laughing along with them at something Lane was saying. Boomer, Case's shepherd and black Lab mix, who had fallen as hard for Gwen as his human did, was with them, too. One of the guys who worked for the tree service was keeping him for the weekend, but he'd brought him for the ceremony. He even had a dapper bow tie that matched Case's, since he'd be standing with him and Lane during the ceremony.

Molly paused for a moment, watching them. It was too bad they weren't *really* a couple because it was nice to have found a man who fit so easily into her friend group.

The last guy she'd dated didn't want kids, which wasn't a problem, obviously. Neither did she. But she hadn't known he actively *disliked* kids until she'd realized he was slowly cutting Mallory and her boys out of Molly's life by avoiding the Sutton house and "accidentally" making plans on the same day as events the family was having. As soon as she caught on, he was history. The guy before that hadn't gelled with Lane or Case, and he'd been a jerk about it.

Callan seemed to get along with them in a way that wasn't forced or just for Molly's benefit. He liked them, especially Irish, who he talked to at the taproom a lot. He didn't know Case or Lane quite as well, but he was getting there.

And damn, the man looked good in a suit.

They were all attractive, of course. And Case and Lane looked incredible in their tuxes. But it was Callan who drew and kept her gaze, and she was getting used to that brief moment of breathlessness whenever he turned and their eyes met.

We're both adults.

She wished she was brave enough to just ask him straight-out what he'd meant by that, but she couldn't do it before the wedding. If he'd meant they were adult enough to share a bed in a platonic way, she'd be disappointed. She felt things like that too deeply to risk it ruining such a happy day.

Instead, she'd savor the anticipation that came with the other, far less disappointing option.

No matter what he'd meant when he sent the text message, there was nothing platonic about the way Callan was looking at her now.

"Is it time?" Case asked, and the way he looked so happy and ready to do this made Molly smile. No cold feet for this guy.

"Almost. They're having a moment."

Case nodded. She didn't need to explain. She knew they'd had their own moment of missing and honoring David Sutton when they put a boutonniere matching theirs on his chair.

"We should go sit because it won't be long," Molly said. Not necessarily because she was in a hurry, but because she wanted Callan all to herself.

Callan shook Case's hand and then Lane's, and Molly hugged Case and rubbed Boomer's head before Callan reached out to her. She took his hand and they made their way through the inn to the sprawl-

w

ing back lawn where the ceremony would take place under a flower-covered arch, with the lake shimmering behind the bride and groom.

With clear skies, they'd opted out of putting up the canopy, but it was a warm day. Rather than sit in the sun longer than necessary, she led the way to some shade under trees at the corner of the house.

"This is one of the most beautiful wedding venues I've ever seen," Callan said as they watched the guests milling around.

"It really is. I hadn't even heard of it until Gwen showed us the website. It's perfect for them. Elegant without being too fussy or fancy, like them."

"Unlike Becca's outfit," he said, and Molly laughed.

Evie had really gone all out on her infant daughter's wedding outfit. It was a very pale pink, with ruffles and lace. She had a diaper cover that matched, and the headband around her fuzzy hairline had a little tiara sewn in. The small stroller Laura was pushing her around in was decorated with flowers and ribbons that matched the arch and the aisle decorations.

"Laura looks like she's pushing around a little princess," Molly said. "And Laura looks pretty, too."

"Yes, she does. She comes into the library often and she's a very nice woman. It's sad that she lost her husband so young."

"Yeah, it was hard on Lane, too, losing his dad so soon after finishing college and marrying Evie.

The first time, I mean. They got divorced that same year, but now they're married again and have Becca, so it's all good."

"That's a long time for such a lovely woman like Laura to be alone, though."

"It is, but I don't think I've ever heard her talking about wanting to date," Molly said. "And even though she'd be happy for Laura, Ellen would be a little sad to lose her partner in widowhood. Like Thelma without Louise."

Callan snorted. "I don't think enough people remember how that movie ended."

"I've never actually seen it," she admitted. "I should make a note to watch it."

"I'll remind you to make a note to watch it later," he said, nudging her lightly with his arm.

"Honored guests, please take your seats as the groom will be joining us momentarily," a woman said over the speakers hidden throughout the venue.

"I should probably warn you I always cry at weddings," she said as they walked toward the chairs.

He chuckled. "Should I pretend to be surprised?"

They had reserved seats with name cards in the second row, and they were right in front of Molly's parents. Molly knew the guest list had been one of the hardest parts of planning the wedding. With a community the size of Stonefield, it was obvious who got invited to a wedding and who didn't, so they'd kept the list as small as possible without slighting anybody who would expect to be invited.

Molly thought it would be fun to get married in the town square so anybody who wanted to show up would be invited. It could be a potluck, though she'd need a *really* big cake. Probably a dozen of them.

Then the bridal march music swelled and Molly forgot about her imaginary wedding to focus on the very real one happening around her.

The look on Case's face when he saw Gwen in her sleek white gown started the tears welling in Molly's eyes, and the love in Gwen's eyes as she walked down the aisle without taking her eyes off the groom made them spill over onto her cheeks.

When Boomer gave a hearty *woof* and bounded down the aisle to escort Gwen to Case's side, chuckles rippled through the guests.

The tears started falling again when Case and Gwen vowed to love and cherish each other for the rest of their lives, and she was thankful Callan had had the foresight to tuck a pocket pack of tissues into his coat's inside pocket.

She wasn't sure how or when it happened, but around the time Case got to kiss his bride, Molly realized she was holding Callan's hand, their locked fingers resting on his thigh. They stood to watch Case and Gwen walk down the aisle as husband and wife without letting go, and she had to remind herself in a very stern inner voice that he was playing the part of a good boyfriend before she could turn to face him.

"How's my makeup?" she asked, knowing it must be a mess and hoping it would make him laugh.

But he didn't. Instead he brushed a strand of hair away from her face. "You look beautiful."

She could see by the look in his eyes that he wasn't lying. But he also hadn't answered the question. "Is it running? Be honest."

Instead, he took a fresh tissue out of the pack and dabbed gently under her eyes. With the side of his thumb, he wiped gently before dabbing with the tissue again. "There. It's a little bit like that…what do they call it, with all the tutorials and memes online?"

"Smoky eye?" She gave him a skeptical look. "You used a tissue and your thumb to turn my running mascara and eyeliner into smoky eye?"

"I said a *little bit* like smoky eye. A very little bit." When she laughed, he put his arm around her and held her tight. Then he whispered close to her ear, "You do look beautiful. But since I'm a good fake boyfriend, I'll admit you might want to touch it up before people start taking pictures."

Just as Molly was about to tilt her head back and maybe get a quick kiss, she caught Evie watching her. They made eye contact and she could see the question in her friend's eyes as clearly as if she'd spoken it out loud.

Is this still fake or what? Because it doesn't look it.

She looked away because she didn't know the answer—and she didn't want Evie to know that—but she was hyperaware of Callan's hand at her waist as they followed the other guests down the aisle.

Was it still fake? Molly had no idea. But what she wasn't going to do while he was looking so hot in that suit and his hand was on her body was worry about it.

Callan wasn't sure, but it felt like it took longer for the photographer to take pictures after the ceremony than the actual ceremony itself took. Not that he minded because there were cocktails and hors d'oeuvres, plus he had Molly keeping up a running commentary.

"See the way Mallory has her hands folded together like she's all serene? But you can see she's twisting them because she's out of patience and that photographer only has a few more shots before they're down the matron of honor. And see how Irish is hovering and scowling? He's going to insist Mallory sit down and put her feet up, and it's basically a toss-up as to which of them is going to blow first."

Once the posed photography—under the arch, under trees, in the gardens, and pretty much everyplace on the grounds—was over, they moved inside. While the patio doors would be left open so the party could spill outside as people chose, the air-conditioning was on inside, so that was where the rest of the formalities took place.

He had a fresh pack of tissues ready for the bride and groom's first dance. And for the best man's toast. Lane clearly wasn't comfortable with public speaking, but he spoke from the heart and Molly wasn't the only person sniffling. The dinner was outstanding, and then came the moment they'd both been waiting for—the cutting of the cake.

"Do you think it's red velvet?" he leaned close to ask.

"I don't think so. I think it's going to be vanilla, but the other cake—the groom's cake or whatever it's called—will be chocolate."

"You really think Mallory would get excited about vanilla cake?"

"It's hard to say. A really good vanilla cake is underrated, you know. Just like vanilla ice cream. Everybody gets so distracted by a whole sign filled with a hundred different flavors and forgets that a simple vanilla cone can be the perfect thing."

She never failed to surprise him. He would have guessed Molly would be the first to go for one of the multicolored ice creams that mashed trendy flavors together just because it was fun.

The wedding cake turned out to be a surprisingly delicious orange cream cake, though there was both a vanilla and a chocolate layer for those who preferred them. Callan didn't prefer those because the orange cream was delicious.

"Do you know which bakery made this cake?" he

asked Molly when they'd finished their slices and he'd had to restrain himself from licking the crumbs off the plate.

"No, but I can find out." Molly leaned close to lower her voice. "Or I can cheat and announce that nobody could possibly duplicate a cake like that while Ellen and Laura are within earshot. They'll have a recipe within a week."

Once the cake was cleared, the reception turned the corner into a straight-up party. Ellen and Laura each kissed the bride and groom before taking the kids back to the suite. Some of the guests said their goodbyes—including Paul and Amanda Cyrs— and Callan assumed the rest would leave in a constant trickle. A few would probably stay to the end, though, and get back to Stonefield late.

And then he would be sharing a bed with Molly.

"I'm going to go dance," Molly said, pushing back her chair and standing.

When she gave him a questioning look, he shook his head. "Go have fun."

And she definitely did. She danced with the same joy she did everything she enjoyed. He couldn't take his eyes off her as she danced with her friends, all of them laughing and shimmying and clearly having the time of their lives.

For the first time in his life, Callan regretted never having learned to dance. It didn't matter if it was ballroom or a night out at the club, he had no rhythm and didn't need anybody to tell him he looked utterly ridiculous if he tried. He'd never cared. He didn't really spend much time in ballrooms or nightclubs.

Watching Molly on the dance floor, though, had him *yearning* to join her. In that moment, he'd give anything to be able to move his body in a rhythm that complemented hers. He wanted his hands on her hips and her arms around his neck as she rested her head against his shoulder.

"Go dance with her."

Callan turned to Irish, who'd apparently taken a seat at the table without him noticing. "I can't dance. I never learned how."

"It doesn't matter."

Callan laughed. "It'll matter when I look like a drunken clown out there and step all over her feet."

The other man barely cracked a smile. "Trust me, it doesn't matter at all. I didn't think I could dance, either, but there was an event at the taproom one night and I could tell Mallory really wanted to dance, so I danced with her."

"Did you look ridiculous?"

"Don't know. Don't care." Irish tipped his head slightly. "Once I had Mallory in my arms, we just kind of swayed with the music and all that mattered was that I was holding her and she was smiling."

The words were barely out of Irish's mouth before the music changed. As the thumping dance tune segued into a ballad, he saw the disappointment in Molly as the people around her started pairing off.

The realization some other guy might step up and sweep her into his arms got Callan to his feet. And wanting to put that smile back on her face got him moving.

She was almost to the edge of the dance floor when she saw him coming, and her face lit up in a way that made the impending humiliation one-hundred-percent worth it. Whenever her gaze locked on his and she smiled, it was like sunshine breaking through the clouds. Molly was the pot of gold at the end of the rainbow.

Even with anxiety knotting his stomach, he bowed slightly because it would make her laugh and extended his hand. "May I have this dance?"

Molly put her hand in his and dropped into a curtsy that would have put a Regency lady to shame. "It would be my pleasure."

After rising, she tugged him into the crowd of couples slow-dancing, and the joy in her eyes when she looked up at him tightened the knot.

"I should warn you, I... I can't dance," he admitted, expecting her happiness to dim slightly.

If anything, it got brighter. She ran her hands up his arms until they clasped behind his neck. This brought her body tantalizingly close to his, and his hands went to her hips without conscious thought on his part.

"Dancing is easy," she said as her hips swayed gently. "You just hold me really, *really* close and relax your body."

He did as he was told, and the anxiety knot in his stomach loosened as his body started naturally swaying with hers.

"Everybody else seems to be spinning in circles," he said, glancing around at the other couples. "Shouldn't we be doing that?"

She let go of his neck long enough to take his chin and tip his face back to hers. "We can dance however we want."

And they did. He held her really close, his body relaxed and following Molly's lead. She leaned her head against his chest, and he inhaled the sweet scent of her hair. And regret flooded him when he recognized the old ballad was winding down.

Molly lifted her head. "I heard somebody say the chicken dance is next."

He laughed. "I am *not* doing the chicken dance."

"Thank you for dancing with me, Callan," she said, and then she stood on her toes to give him a fast, hard kiss. "But if you don't escape in the next fifteen seconds, you *will* get dragged into the chicken dance."

He didn't run, but he left the dance floor like there was a gold medal for speed walking waiting for him on the other side. Irish was laughing at him when he got back to the table, and Callan shook his head before taking a long drink of water.

"You were right," he told the cowboy while they watched the majority of the remaining guests gleefully dance like chickens. "It was worth it."

"Told you."

"But you opted out of this one."

Irish snorted and nodded his head toward Mallory, who was flapping like a very pregnant hen. "I love that woman with my whole soul and I'd give my life for her, but I won't dance like a chicken."

As the evening wound to a close, there was one tradition left to honor, and Callan stood in a corner with the groom, Lane, Irish and a few other guys while Gwen took her place in front of the head table. All of the single women who were left spread out across the dance floor.

"Okay, ladies," the wedding planner supplied by the venue said. "Tradition says the woman who catches the bouquet will be the next bride, so get ready!"

As Gwen turned her back on the single, female guests, dread hit Callan's stomach like a lead ball. People not only accepted he was dating Molly, but they embraced it. Even the people who knew the truth seemed to act like they were really a couple. If she caught that bouquet, there was going to be a lot of talk about her being a bride soon. Once that seed was planted in people's minds, extricating themselves from the ruse would be even more complicated.

He watched Gwen count down from three and then she tossed the bouquet. It went high, making a perfect arc in Molly's direction.

Oh no. No no no.

She caught it like it was a game-winning touchdown, and when he heard the men chuckling and saw the glares a few of the women gave him, he realized he'd made the plea out loud.

And everybody had heard him.

Chapter Thirteen

*Thanks to a typo on the order form they sub-
mitted to their supplier, Dearborn's Market
has asked us to let you all know you can buy
a whole lot of peaches for not a whole lot of
money. Bakers, canners and fruit lovers, stop
by the market to get fresh peaches at a deeply
discounted price while supplies last!*
—Stonefield Gazette *Facebook Page*

They were almost to her room—or to *their* room,
actually—when Molly's phone vibrated. Usually she
couldn't resist the compulsion to respond to her no-
tifications, but right now she didn't want to be distracted away from Callan. If it was an emergency,
the unanswered text message would be followed by

a phone call. Then she'd look because her aversion to using her cell phone as an actual telephone was well-known so she knew it would be urgent.

As far as Molly was concerned, the only thing urgent at the moment was her need to get Callan on the other side of a do-not-disturb sign.

He'd apologized for his reaction to her catching Gwen's bouquet several times since they left the reception, even though she kept telling him she'd thought it was funny. Everybody had, really. At the time, she'd mostly been wondering if she could find statistics online for how often women who caught wedding bouquets actually were the next bride. She thought it was probably very few, but it would be a fun thing to research.

Once it was time to call it a night, though, all of her focus had gone straight to the king-size bed waiting for them.

We're both adults.

"I can't believe I did that," he said for the fourth or fifth time. She was losing count.

After hanging the do-not-disturb sign on the outside of the door, she closed it and flipped the security bar. Then she slipped her shoes off with a relieved sigh and tossed her small clutch and the bouquet on the antique writing desk.

His gaze fell on the bouquet and she saw his shoulders stiffen. He really wasn't going to give up on that. "Callan. Seriously. Let the bouquet thing go. It was funny. Everybody laughed."

"When a man sounds horrified at the thought of his girlfriend being the next bride, that's rude. It might be funny, but it's also rude." He ran a hand over his hair. "And also, if people start getting ideas about our future, it makes the end of our relationship that much messier."

"We've only been fake dating for a little over a month. They would think it was weird if you *did* want to think about marriage already. And also, people are *not* getting ideas about us." Maybe *she* was, but she didn't say that part out loud.

"A few women gave me dirty looks," he said.

"Of course they did, but we don't care." She sighed. "Clearly you need a distraction. Come unzip me."

Whatever he'd been about to say—probably *I can't believe I did that* for the fifth or sixth time—must have gotten stuck, judging by the way his Adam's apple bobbed as he swallowed hard.

"Callan." She couldn't believe she was going to have to ask him twice. She turned her back and then looked at him over her shoulder to emphasize the point. "Can you unzip me, please?"

When his fingertips brushed the skin just above the zipper, Molly closed her eyes and let the thrill of his touch wash over her. Those fingertips stayed as his other hand tugged down the zipper, and then he skimmed them down the center of her spine.

"This is a bad idea."

She chuckled. "I think we've already established that I never let an idea being bad stop me."

He slid both hands in the gap of the dress, then moved them up to her shoulders and out, pushing the dress down her arms. Then his mouth was on the back of her neck and she knew they wouldn't be making a wall out of the extra pillows tonight.

"You're a terrible influence on me," he said against her skin.

"Consider it method acting. Total immersion in the role."

"I like the way you think, Molly Cyrs."

The joke about never having heard *that* before died on her lips when he put his arm around her waist and pulled her back against his body. He was hard and he moaned when she moved her hips to grind against him.

They took their time peeling the wedding clothes off each other, pausing frequently for slow, deep kisses that she never wanted to end. But it was hard to remove clothing while kissing, so his mouth would break away from hers and clothes would hit the floor and then his mouth would claim hers again.

His hands on her naked skin was Molly's new favorite thing ever, except maybe for her hands on *his* naked body. They explored every inch of each other—touching and licking and occasionally gently nipping—until Molly's need for him was so intense she was trembling.

She'd stashed some condoms on the nightstand earlier in the day, and after spending some time between her thighs, teasing her mercilessly with his tongue, Callan finally slipped one on.

He said her name in a low, rough voice as he entered her, and she dug her fingertips into his upper arms as he thrust slowly—a little deeper each time until he filled her.

Molly lost herself in the sensation of Callan—his breath on her jaw as he whispered how good she felt and the sheen of sweat as she ran her nails down his back. The sweet friction as he moved within her, his pace quickening as she moaned and clutched his arms.

Her orgasm shook her and she said his name as she clutched the duvet in her fists. He thrust harder and her back arched off the bed as wave after wave of pleasure washed over her.

She let go of the duvet and ran her hands down his back until her hands cupped the curve of his ass. Molly urged him on and he groaned as he found his own release. He buried his face in her neck, his breath hot and fast against her skin, until the tremors passed.

Still catching her breath, Molly buried her fingers in his hair and gently scratched at his scalp. The sound of pleasure he made sounded exactly like purring and a giggle escaped her before she could stifle it.

"I can't believe you're laughing at me right now," he muttered against her skin.

"I'm sorry, but you sounded like a cat. You literally purred."

"I did not." She scraped her fingernails through his hair and he made the sound again. "Okay. I hear it now."

When he rolled off her, Molly slid out of the bed. "Be right back. Gotta pee."

Callan had managed to get himself under the duvet by the time she returned from the bathroom. She could tell just by looking at him that he was on the verge of sleep, but she took a minute to turn off the lights and plug in their phones.

When she slid back into bed, he pulled her up against him and kissed her hair. "I like this method acting thing."

"Me too. Really elevates our faking game."

"But not everything was fake, right?" he asked, actually sounding anxious about the answer. She said nothing, and he nudged her a little. "Right?"

She laughed and let him off the hook. "Definitely *not* fake."

A few minutes later, she could tell by the way his breathing changed that he'd fallen asleep. She was exhausted after a long, wonderful day topped off by

an orgasm, but sleep had never come easily to Molly.
And there was still that uncleared notification.

She knew picking her phone up was the worst
possible thing to do when it was time to at least try
to go to sleep, but she couldn't help it. Using the
duvet to shield the screen so the light wouldn't dis-
turb Callan, she unlocked her phone to find a text
message from Evie.

Molly Cyrs, do NOT have sex with Callan.

Oops.

It had been a very long time since Callan had
awakened naked, with half his body hot from the
woman pressed along it and the other half cold because she'd stolen the covers, and unable to feel his
hand because she was on his arm.

It was a lot sexier and more romantic in the movies, he thought as he tried to extract his arm without
waking Molly.

It didn't work. With a squeaky sound of alarm,
Molly sat upright, her head jerking back and forth
as she tried to see past the mass of hair she couldn't
push away from her face fast enough.

Then her gaze landed on him and she laughed
before flopping back down onto the pillow. Luckily, he'd moved his arm while he'd had the chance
and was making and releasing a fist over and over
to get the feeling back.

"Good morning," he said. "Do you always wake up like that or were you dreaming somebody was breaking in?"

"I'm not used to something moving in my bed when I'm asleep, I guess."

It was ridiculous how happy those words made him.

"What time is it?" she asked, finally wrangling her hair away from her face so she could see the clock. "Oh no. We have to hurry if we're not going to be late to breakfast."

He didn't want to hurry. He wanted to pull her into his arms and make love to her again. Then he wanted to cuddle and drift back to sleep for a while, but without his arm trapped under her this time.

But she was already sliding out of bed, and then she yelled for him to close his eyes before she ran to the bathroom and slammed the door. He closed his eyes because she told him to and didn't bother reminding her he'd already seen every gorgeous inch of her.

By the time she came out of the bathroom, he'd already taken what would technically be considered a nap, he guessed. He'd nodded off and woke up to what sounded like something heavy being dropped in the hallway. Somebody's luggage he assumed.

"Callan!" she said when she stepped back into the room. "You're not ready."

"I've been waiting for my turn in the bathroom,"

he pointed out. "Since you're wearing a towel, which I assume isn't what you're wearing to breakfast, I'll probably still be ready before you."

She beat him by three minutes, which she lorded over him as they navigated through the inn to the cozy dining room where they were meeting the others for a post-wedding breakfast before they all headed home.

When they entered, every head turned in their direction. Ellen and Laura smiled and said good morning, but he could see the speculation on the others' faces as their gazes bounced between him and Molly as if one of them might be wearing a T-shirt that said "I had sex last night" or something.

It was a buffet breakfast, so they filled plates before joining the others at the long wooden table. Everybody was there except the newlyweds.

The topic of conversation was the wedding, of course, so Callan was quiet while he ate. And he tried to keep his eyes on his plate for the most part, but he also couldn't be awkward about it, so he didn't miss *all* of the looks passing between Molly and the other women, and then the other women and their men, and then the men looking at him.

"Oh, you have to try this," Molly said, offering him what looked like a spinach quiche on the end of her fork.

They really were too good at this fake dating thing for their own good, he thought. But he sampled the quiche from her fork and had to admit it was delicious. He offered her a bite of his bread pudding and before he knew it, she'd shifted her chair and plate closer to his so they could share everything.

"Callan, did you have fun last night?" Ellen asked, and half the table almost choked on whatever they had in their mouths at that moment.

"I…" He had no idea what to say. "Yes?"

That seemed to be the right answer because she gave him a warm smile. "I know weddings can be overwhelming, but I think you knew almost everybody who was here."

"Almost everybody," he agreed, and then he shoved a huge forkful of scrambled eggs into his mouth so he wouldn't have to talk anymore.

Becca, who was sitting on Evie's lap while she ate one-handed, started to fuss, and before Laura or Ellen could offer to take the baby, Molly was on her feet.

"Come see Auntie Molly," she cooed, taking Becca off Evie's lap and blowing a raspberry kiss on her cheek.

Callan did his best to focus on his plate, but his awareness of how adorable Molly looked with Becca was brutal.

They'd held hands. Laughed. Danced. Made love. Woke up together. Everybody in their lives seemed to accept them to the point nobody—including him—was sure if they were even faking anymore.

But Molly bouncing a baby on her knee and talking to her in a singsong voice was almost a physical blow—like a slap to the face to bring him back to reality. Right next to him was the picture of something he wanted desperately in his life. And he wanted *real* children, which would require a *real* relationship, not a fake one.

They lingered at the breakfast table until Irish pointed out they were going to be cutting it close to checkout time. Everybody scrambled and after kissing the top of her head, Molly reluctantly handed Becca back to her mother.

"You're really good with babies," he told her as they rushed to finish packing. Maybe he was fishing, trying to find a side door into the status of their relationship because he didn't have the courage to breach the subject head-on.

"I love kids," she said easily, zipping up her suitcase. "But it's a lot easier when you're an auntie and not a mom. I can only do so much damage."

The odd phrasing stuck out to him. A lot of people said they liked being an auntie or an uncle and then gave them back to the parents for dirty diapers and temper tantrums and teething. But she'd said she could only do so much damage and he didn't know what that meant.

But they had to go, so he didn't get to push the conversation any further. Gwen had sent a lecture by way of Mallory about the additional costs they'd incur if everybody didn't get out when they were supposed to.

The long round of goodbyes and hugs in the parking lot amused Callan because they were all about to get in their vehicles and they were all going in the same direction. But he was catching on to how this family did things and he accepted the hugs and handshakes before picking up their bags and following Molly to where she'd parked her car.

Her very tiny and very yellow convertible.

"I'm not sure the luggage and I will all fit," he said, eyeing the lack of space. "Maybe if you put the top down I won't have to ride hunched over."

"You told me you thought it was cute and very me," she reminded him.

"When I said that, I didn't know I'd have to ride for over an hour folded up in the passenger seat."

"You're not *that* tall. And the shape of the car built around the front seats might be small, but I think the actual seats and stuff are all a standard size."

"They are not."

"You can ride back with Ellen and Laura if you want. They love having somebody to talk to. Or you can go with Evie and Lane. You can sit in the back seat and keep Becca company." She shrugged. "Irish and Mallory have Jack and Eli, but they'll probably have their faces glued to their phones or whatever video game thing they brought. But still a good option if you want to stop every ten minutes so Mallory can pee."

"I guess maybe I'll fit," he conceded, and then once he'd stowed the luggage and lowered himself into the passenger seat, he had to admit he'd been wrong. It was definitely more spacious on the inside than it looked from the outside.

As they pulled out onto the main street behind Lane and Ellen's vehicles, Molly hit the button on her steering wheel to cycle through radio stations until she found a song she wanted to sing along to.

Callan was content to ride in silence as he processed everything that had happened between them in the last twenty-four hours. Even though they hadn't talked about it, spending the night together had to have changed everything. They'd crossed a line and he didn't see any way they could continue on with this charade without crossing it again. And he wanted to cross it. He wanted the line between the ruse and reality to fade away to nothing.

But he wasn't sure about Molly. In some ways, she was incapable of not showing every emotion she felt. But he'd noticed that there were times only a person *really* paying attention and aware that everything wasn't sunshine and rainbows with her would be able to tell she was hiding how she felt. He had no way of knowing if she actually still believed they were only pretending to be a couple, or if she didn't want him to know her feelings for him were becoming real.

Then he thought about how it felt to watch her holding Becca. His emotional response in that moment told him everything he needed to know about whether or not his feelings were still fake.

He didn't want to pretend anymore. This thing he and Molly had going on was the best thing that had ever happened to him, and he didn't want to let it go.

Chapter Fourteen

It's comedy open mic night at Sutton's Place Brewery & Tavern! Remember, if you're brave enough to take the stage, you get your choice of a free beer or a free order of nachos! Just remember to keep it clean and if you tell a funny story that happens to be inspired by real events, you should change the names to protect the easily embarrassed!
—Stonefield Gazette *Facebook Page*

"I can't believe I let you talk me into this," Callan said as he followed Molly through the taproom door. "I should be working on my house."

"This will be much more fun. Trust me."

Everything was more fun when compared to home

renovation, but he thought tonight might test that theory. In his experience, amateur open mic comedy was an exercise in not letting anybody see you cringe. He'd met most of the residents of Stonefield at this point, and he wasn't sure he needed to see a steady stream of them trying to make dating woes and the trials of parenthood funny. Or even worse, regurgitating acts from their favorite comics, but with one-hundred-percent less stage presence and no comedic timing.

"I pretty much trusted you with my entire livelihood," he reminded her. "This might be asking too much, though."

"Free nachos, Callan. You get up there, tell some jokes and they give you free nachos. It's literally my favorite thing."

He chuckled as they made their way to the end of the bar, where two stools had reserved signs on them. Everything was her literal favorite thing in the moment. "Are you sure we can sit here? It says these are reserved."

"They are," she said, hopping onto one of the stools. "For us. I asked Lane to put a sign on them because it gets busy on comedy night and I didn't want to miss getting a spot."

"A spot?"

"It's open mic night," she said, holding up her hands as if it was obvious. "If I can't get in, I can't get a spot."

"Wait, you're actually going up there?"

"I've done it before and people laughed. And nobody threw rotten vegetables at me or anything."

"Do the people in Stonefield usually bring rotten vegetables with them to bars? I mean, not that that's the reason they're not throwing them at you. Just wondering."

"I haven't seen any, but Mrs. Flanders carries a *very* big purse and I've never seen her open it."

He covered her hand with his. "Tell you what. If I see Mrs. Flanders opening her purse while you're up there, I'll throw myself on it."

She laughed and leaned close to bump his shoulder with hers. "Do you even know who Mrs. Flanders is?"

"No, but I'll be watching for a woman opening a *very* big purse. Or maybe any purse, just in case somebody brought something small. I'd hate to see you get taken out by a rotten radish."

"What a great *Gazette* post that would be, though." She grinned and covered his hand with hers. "I'll share my free beer and nachos with you."

"Maybe he should go up there and earn his own free beer," Irish said, setting a coaster in front of each of them.

Callan laughed. "Maybe *you* should go up there because you're a really funny guy."

"While you're here, we ran the numbers on the Books & Brews event and we'd like to make that a monthly thing if you're up to it. Having one big Wednesday night per month is a nice bump without really adding to anybody's workload." The cowboy grinned. "Except yours."

According to Molly, they'd chosen a Wednesday night because it was significantly less busy than their other nights. Not only did a lot of people get paid on Thursdays, but the taproom's original hours had been Thursday through Sunday. Once Irish had joined the team—and the family—they'd added Wednesdays, but they tended to be slow.

They'd had the inaugural Books & Brews event here three nights before and they'd gotten more of a crowd than Callan had anticipated. The discussion had been *very* lively, even drawing in a few customers sitting at the bar who hadn't even read the book. They'd all agreed they'd like to do it again, and they'd already picked their next book before he had a chance to tell them they had to run it by Irish and the other owners first.

"I think it would be great to do monthly," he said. It wasn't as though he had an overflowing social calendar, and the more the community saw value in the library, the better. "They want to do another book to movie, I guess."

"Because it made for a lively discussion," Molly sang, doing a little dance on her stool that made both men laugh. "Ha! Made you laugh, Irish."

"You don't get free nachos unless you take the stage."

"And speaking of the stage, Evie just waved me up, so go ahead and start heating that cheese, my friend."

She hopped off the stool and winked at Callan before hurrying to where Evie stood in front of the glass wall with a microphone. As she walked through the crowd, scattered applause and a few cheers broke out, and Callan turned on his stool so he could face that direction. This was a side of Molly he hadn't seen-yet and he was intrigued.

"I won't bother with an introduction," Evie said into the microphone. "Here she is—our own Molly Cyrs!"

Molly took the microphone and waited for the clapping to die down before she started talking. She looked so confident and Callan couldn't believe nobody had ever mentioned this aspect of her life.

"So I have a boyfriend now," Molly said, and more applause and a few whistles rippled through the crowd. "Yeah, he's pretty great. He's the librarian now and—"

Loud applause and cheers interrupted her and Callan fought an urge to vault over the bar and hide behind it. Instead he gave a little wave to the crowd while Molly waited for them to calm down.

"He was my plus-one to the Sutton-Danforth wedding recently." She paused. Shook her head. "Ladies, let me tell you, there's nothing less flattering than your boyfriend yelling *no, no, no* over and over as you catch the bouquet."

Callan winced, but she laughed with the crowd, who'd probably already heard the story. But not from Molly, and certainly not at a comedy open mic night.

"He was sorry, of course," she continued. "Especially when he started taking his suit off and I yelled *no, no, no!*"

The crowd liked that one and Callan joined in the good-natured laughter. He was a little relieved when she went off on a new subject, though—talking about the reactions you got when you took a hearse through a drive-through. He laughed along with the crowd as she finished her bit, and then joined in the resounding applause when she handed the microphone back to Evie. When he saw Molly was heading for the restroom, he turned back to the bar.

Irish set a fresh pour in front of him, even though he hadn't asked for one. "I was busy earlier and forgot, but I switched out your glass. This one's on the house."

"Hey!" Molly said, climbing back onto her stool. "I have to work for my free beer, but you're just giving them away?"

"Work?" Irish laughed and swung the bar towel over his shoulder before walking away.

Callan ran his thumb over his name, which was etched into the glass under the three lupines making up the Sutton's Place logo. He was a regular now. A member of the community with his own glass at the town's favorite hangout spot.

"Oh!" Molly exclaimed, peering over his hand. "You got a glass!"

"I guess I belong now," he said in a voice that was rougher with emotion than he'd intended.

She leaned close, her upper arm pressed to his. "I told you our plan made perfect sense."

"You were right."

She grinned. "There's something I don't get to hear every day."

"How about a movie night tomorrow night?" he asked, because tonight had been enjoyable, but he'd like to spend some quiet time alone together.

Molly blinked. "I like movies, but it's a half hour to the closest movie theater."

"I was thinking more like a movie night at my place. Something streaming or rented. Microwave popcorn. We've watched a few shows together, but we haven't had a movie night."

A movie night sounded more like a date. A *real* date, and not one that would put them out in public where they could show off their relationship to the good people of Stonefield. It was a bad idea. He knew that. The best way to find his way out of this tangled web they'd woven was not to tangle himself up further. But he just wanted a quiet, relaxed evening with her.

"Okay. A movie night sounds fun," she said.

"I'll add microwave popcorn to my shopping list." He turned his head toward her, lowering it so their faces were very close together, but not quite close enough to kiss. "You were incredible up there. I knew you were funny, but I had no idea you're *that* funny."

"I should have run it by you first, but I was afraid you wouldn't come. You're not offended, are you?"

"Of course not. I understand how comedy works, and you do it brilliantly."

Her eyes sparkled as she picked up the glass Irish had put in front of her at some point. "Thank you. Here's to us both being awesome."

When he lifted his glass to clink it against hers, his gaze was drawn to the etched names on each. *Molly. Callan.* They looked good together.

"Cheers."

They decided movie night would have to be at Molly's place, since his bathroom was half torn apart and he said he'd be embarrassed for her to be in there. After he locked up the library, she met him at the diner for a quick bite to eat since his kitchen was also a bit of a mess, as were her cooking skills. And neither of them wanted to join Paul and Amanda for whatever they were having.

Molly couldn't avoid her mother. They lived kind of together and they worked together. And she loved the woman with her whole heart, but she wasn't ready to sit at the dinner table, hypersensitive to every look her mother gave her or Callan. Molly wasn't sure if she didn't like the idea of them dating or if she liked the idea *too* much, but she wasn't in the mood to try to dissect her mother's facial expressions.

She could feel the annoyance rising again and deliberately pushed thoughts of her mom out of her head. It was movie night with Callan and that was all she was going to think about right now.

"Was there anything in particular you wanted to watch?" he asked once they were settled in her apartment.

"Not really," Molly said, and she could feel her body tensing. Here it came.

What do you want to watch? I don't know, what do you want to watch? And she'd be trying to think of every movie she'd ever heard of and think of one she wanted to watch, but only if she thought it might be one he wanted to watch, too. And the pressure of trying to come up with a movie she thought they both might like would ramp up her anxiety until she was cranky and snapped at him and ruined the entire night.

"Okay." He nodded and held up a sticky note. "I wrote down three movies I'd like to see, so tell me if one jumps out at you. If not, we'll write them on separate sticky notes, fold them up, put them in a bowl and pick one. And that's what we'll watch. I was thinking *Thelma & Louise*, though."

"Yes." She was stunned—in a good way—and she tried to think of something to say that would distract her from collapsing into relieved sobs. "I find sticky notes incredibly sexy. Just so you know."

His eyebrow arched. "You find sticky notes sexy? Or you find the *use* of sticky notes to be sexy?"

"I find you with your sticky note in particular to be sexy. Is this how you usually choose a movie?"

"No, not really." When she continued to watch him, trying to figure him out, his cheeks turned pink. "I was reading about ADHD and decision fatigue, and I pay attention to you, so I've seen it happening. I just thought this would make it easier."

Tears filled her eyes and she laughed as she wiped them away. "I don't know why I'm almost crying."

"I'm glad I didn't choose the *throw darts at the sticky notes* method if your vision's going to be all blurry."

"There are people who tolerate me and some totally accept me, but you might be the first person to go out of your way to actually accommodate me—to navigate the ADHD in a way that makes it easier for me."

He reached out and took her hand, giving it a little squeeze. "It just takes a little research and you may not know this about me, but I'm a bit of a book nerd."

"Callan Avery," she said in a breathy way, exag-

gerated for effect. "A book nerd with sticky notes.
Are you trying to get me naked?"

"Is it working? Because I can run back to my
place for page flags and highlighters if I need to
step up my game."

"Oh, it's working." She was definitely getting
naked with him tonight. "But this is the best movie
night ever, so I want to enjoy it first."

He chuckled. "You haven't seen the movie yet.
What if it sucks?"

"I don't care. It'll still be the best movie night
ever. And I'll still get naked."

"Good." He reached for the remote with the hand
not holding hers, which he didn't seem inclined to release. She didn't mind at all. "You know, if you keep
a list on your phone of movies you want to watch and
I do the same, we can look for overlap."

"If you keep this up, I'll let *you* get naked, too."

He laughed and hit Play.

A little less than an hour into the movie, Callan
paused it. "What's the matter. Don't you like it?"

Molly's face flamed. "Yes. It's a good movie."

"It's paused, so do you have to pee? You've been
squirming."

"No." Molly sighed, resigned to yet another con-
fession of not being able to do something the way everybody else did. "It's hard for me to sit still and stare
at the television and be quiet for two hours, no matter
how much I'm enjoying the movie. That's why it's

easier to watch shows. The commercials give me a chance to talk and move around every few minutes."

The look he gave her wasn't one of confusion or annoyance, but interest. "What do you usually do while you're watching something?"

"I'll do jigsaw puzzles or color with the app on my tablet, or play a game on my phone. Sometimes I knit. "She pointed to the folded blanket made of brightly colored knit squares over the back of a chair. "That's my *Game of Thrones* blanket."

"So knit something. Or color."

Molly gave him a little shrug. "It seems a little rude."

"I mean, if I'm having a movie night with somebody and they're just on their tablet, I'd assume they don't like the movie. Or me, maybe. But now that you've told me doing something with your hands helps you enjoy the movie more, which is what I want, you should go for it."

"I like to talk sometimes, too. About what's happening on the screen."

"Like color commentary?" When she nodded, he chuckled. "I don't mind, as long as you're not offended if I don't respond because I'm more of a mono-tasker and if I'm focused on the movie, I might not even hear you."

She grinned. "It's a deal."

"Here's another deal—if we're doing something

and changing the way we're doing it makes it easier or more enjoyable for you, just tell me."

Her throat was clogged with emotion, so she nodded and he rewarded her with a warm smile before hitting Play. She reached into the basket at the end of the couch and pulled out the scarf she was working on. She didn't do a lot with patterns while watching things because she always lost her place. But if she lost track with a scarf or blanket square, she could simply go back and count how many stitches were on the needle.

Only three stitches later, he paused the movie again. "So movie theaters must be hard, huh?"

She nodded. "I don't go often because there's so much pressure to be still and quiet. And it's dark, so no phone or knitting. Plus they set the volume so high and I have some sensory issues. I have to be absolutely *dying* to see a movie to see it in a theater because it's so… I don't know. Confining. It's like being in invisible restraints."

"Movies at home are better, anyway. The theaters won't pause the projector if you have to pee, and they get pretty testy if you try to use their microwave."

If they had *really* been dating, Molly would have known right that second that Callan was *the one*. She'd finally found a man who seemed willing and able to roll with the punches her ADHD threw at them with grace and humor.

It was too bad their relationship was fake and, with Old Home Day in less than a week, almost over.

Chapter Fifteen

Once again we want to thank D&T Tree Service for sprucing up the town square and the trees along Main Street in anticipation of the upcoming Old Home Day celebration! They do this wonderful service for our community every year, and we're grateful they made it a priority even though Case Danforth just returned from his honeymoon and Lane Thompson has a little one at home. The people of Stonefield appreciate you!

—Stonefield Gazette *Facebook Page*

Molly grimaced as she filled out her daily sticky note. Today's must-do task of changing out the rugs was one of her least favorites. It was exhausting and, even worse, it required her mother's assistance, so they'd be spending the day together.

Every year around this time, they changed all the carpet runners and area rugs to what Amanda called *the summer rugs*, which were the same basic floral design as the winter ones, but in much lighter colors. They suited the decor much better, but her mother had learned a long time ago that winter boots and light floral designs weren't a great match. So there were darker designs in a coarser knap for snow and mud seasons, and then Molly and her mother would switch them all out for the prettier ones. She'd gotten the text message from Amanda yesterday letting her know she'd blocked off the day for this task.

That sucked, but at least she was going to see Callan first. They were going to meet on the sidewalk in a few minutes and walk to the Perkin' Up Café. And he'd built in some extra time before the library had to open so they could sit down and linger over coffee together. And it had been his suggestion, which was nice.

Callan was waiting for her outside the garage and the way he smiled when he saw her made her pulse quicken. Her pulse had been doing that a lot since the kiss good-night, and it practically raced every time she thought about doing it again.

He held out his hand and she laced her fingers through his, as though there was no doubt they'd be holding hands as they walked. It made her smile because a lot of the couples she knew that *weren't* fake didn't hold hands as much as she and Callan did. It made the line between real and fake seem even fuzzier, but she certainly didn't want to stop.

Maybe she'd worry less about the line if keeping herself from crossing it didn't feel like such a big deal. No matter how much she liked spending time with Callan, especially in bed, though not only there, one thing kept poking at her.

"When we first met, you said you chose Stonefield because it seems like a great community to raise a family," she said, thinking the conversation would be easier if they were side by side and not face-to-face. "So that's part of your plans for your future, then? Kids and all that?"

"Yes. The move to Stonefield. Buying a house to fix up rather than renting an apartment. It's the start of the next phase of my life and being a father is hopefully going to be a big part of it. I want a big family. I want kids—at least two—so they always have somebody in life."

And there it was—the splash of icy water in her face. Callan was going to marry a woman who wanted children. Not just because it was something most people assumed would be a part of their future, but to fill a deep-seated need inside of him. He had no family and he wanted one.

"I made the decision a long time ago to not have kids," she said quietly.

He stopped walking. He didn't let go of her hand or look down at her, but he froze as if he'd walked into a brick wall and didn't know what to do. She wasn't great at judging time, but it felt like a solid minute of stillness before he looked down at her. She couldn't read his expression at all, which made her stomach hurt. Maybe this wasn't a conversation that she should have jumped into so spontaneously.

"You don't have to tell me," he said, softly, "but I'm curious why."

"There's a more than fifty percent chance my child would have ADHD and I refuse to have a baby knowing that baby's life is going to be so hard. And yes, I know there are a lot of gifts that come with being neurodiverse, but working twice as hard to do even the most basic and fundamental things sucks."

He started walking again and since he was still holding her hand, she did, too. "I haven't known you long, but I have a really hard time imagining my life without you in it, with your mermaid sweaters and Molly-ese language substitutions. I think a little version of Molly would be just as adorable."

It was a kind sentiment and she wanted to believe it so badly, but it was also an empty one. "That's because you don't have to depend on me. Someday some poor guy will be sitting in the dark because I forgot to the pay the electric bill, trying to decide if putting expired milk in his coffee will kill him and waiting for the power to come back on because I haven't done laundry in two weeks."

Callan sighed, and she dared to glance sideways at him. He didn't look annoyed or amused. Just thoughtful. "Maybe he should have paid the electric bill and bought milk. Or used sticky notes on the fridge where they couldn't be missed."

"I know there are tools. But you also don't know what it feels like to constantly be disappointing people for your entire life." She stopped walking again, needing a second, but he just held her hand and waited. "This is where you're going to tell me that an over fifty percent chance my kid would have ADHD means there's an almost fifty percent chance they won't, right? Trust me, I've heard it all before and nothing you can say will change my mind."

Some emotion she couldn't quite place flashed through his eyes, and then he shrugged. "I'm not going to try to change your mind. It's none of my business if you have kids or not."

She nodded and started walking again, falling silent because she wasn't sure what else she could say. Even though they were walking down the sidewalk hand in hand, looking like a couple, they weren't. It really *wasn't* his business if she wanted children or not, no matter what, but the urge to explain was still strong. She wasn't sure she could make him understand, though, and it wouldn't be long before they reached the café, so she kept her mouth shut.

It wasn't really that she didn't want to be a mother. Every time she was around kids, that internal clock ticked. She kind of *did* want kids. But then memories of her own childhood would echo through her head. Why did you do that? *I don't know.* Why can't you finish this? *I don't know.* You're so smart, so why can't you finish your assignments? *I don't know.* Why can't you just apply yourself? *I'm trying.* What is wrong with you?

I. Don't. Know.

There was no way she would subject a child to that voluntarily. And sure, maybe she could sympathize with the child, but how was that going to be of any help? It took every drop of executive function she could muster to get through each day without something unraveling. And she managed pretty well because she'd learned how her brain worked and used methods to support her brain chemistry. She also didn't have a lot of pressure because she worked for her parents and lived over their garage. She worked really hard at finding her own balance in life. How was she supposed to help a child navigate the world?

It was better for everybody if she just dedicated herself to being the most awesome aunt ever to Mallory's kids. And Evie's daughter, and any kids Gwen might have. She didn't need to have children of her own to give maternal love, and this way she couldn't mess them up too badly since she didn't have to be in charge of the hard stuff, like feeding them on time and registering them for school and remembering to take them to the pediatrician. Sure, her notebook was a good system for herself, but the consequences for messing up with kids were too high.

"Hey." He tugged at her hand until she looked up at the kind smile he was giving her. "How about I let you choose my coffee this morning?"

Childhood traumas and thoughts of the future scattered like dandelion fuzz and she bounced up and down on her toes. "Do you mean it? Anything? You're not just saying I can order your plain, boring coffee for you, are you?"

"Anything," he said, and then he winced. "No hazelnut or blueberry flavoring, though. I don't like hazelnut and the smell of blueberry coffee turns my stomach."

"This is going to be so fun," she exclaimed, practically dragging him down the sidewalk toward the café. "Trust me, you are going to *love* all the different drinks Chelsea can make. You might never sleep again, but it'll be so worth it. This is going to be the best morning ever!"

Callan was trying to figure out if it was the kitchen floor, the wall or the ceiling that was out of level—or knowing this house, all three, because he hadn't found a square corner yet—when his phone chimed. The text message tone meant it was probably Molly, though he did get messages from other people in town these days, so he set the level down on the temporary worktable he'd made with plywood and two sawhorses, and picked up the phone.

Seeing her name on the screen gave him that familiar burst of pleasure, but it fizzled quickly this time. He'd spent the night tossing and turning, wishing Molly hadn't had plans with the Suttons until late, but also knowing it was probably for the best.

Molly didn't want to have children.

And not in the way some people couldn't imagine themselves as parents, but in a determined and final kind of way. Judging by the conviction in her voice yesterday, she felt as passionately about not having children as he did about someday having them.

A gut-wrenching truth had kept him awake until the wee hours—it was for the best that they'd never had a conversation about how very real their fake relationship had become. It didn't matter now because he couldn't see any way for them to have a future together.

With a knot in his throat, he read her text message.

We'll be hosting a funeral on Thursday evening. There won't be a separate viewing or wake, so just the one night. The obituary isn't written yet, but I wanted to give you advance notice. Also, I'll be busier than usual until it's over.

He'd come to know many of the people in the community, but he didn't ask who had passed. He wasn't sure if they were allowed to talk about it before the obituaries were made public. Not that they were doctors or anything, but it was still a family's deeply personal business.

Thank you for letting me know. Condolences to the family.

He wasn't sure what else he could say, but it seemed enough for Molly. She sent back an emoji that was a smiling face with little hearts, and that was the end of the conversation.

Ten minutes later, it was Rome who set off his phone. Callan sighed as he hit the button to accept the video call. He was never going to get this house done.

"Hey, Rome. What's up?"

"Just checking in. I don't have a lot of time, though."

He never did. "Things are good here."

"Still pretending to date the lady from the funeral home?"

"It's Molly, Rome. You know that. And yes, we're still pretend dating. Though not for much longer.

Rome frowned. "What does even mean, though? And more importantly, are you pretend making out? Pretending to sleep together? It seems like you've been doing this a long time, so what the hell are you doing, man?"

"I'm not answering that." He didn't want to get into that, so instead he talked about the things he and

Molly *had* done together recently, from the Books & Brews event to comedy night. He felt as if the details of them hanging out together might make the whole thing sound less ridiculous to his best friend.

"Callan, you're falling for this woman."

Rome certainly didn't mince words. And he wasn't wrong, but all he had to go on was the vibe Callan gave off when he talked about her. He didn't have all the facts.

"I have fallen for her, Rome. That already happened." Even if he'd wanted to keep that to himself, Rome would see the truth on his face. "I found out yesterday that she doesn't want to have kids, Rome. Ever."

"Damn." Rome's face got smaller as he sat back in his chair. "Do you know why?"

"Yes, and I kind of understand her reasons, even if I don't agree with them. That's her choice to make and she seems pretty set on it."

"You're not thinking about giving up those picket fence dreams, are you?"

Callan sighed. "No. I won't lie—I thought about this all night and all day at work, and I was tempted because if anybody's worth giving them up for, it's her. But I know somewhere down the line, whether it's a year or five or ten, I'd resent not having kids and I'd either push her to change her mind or just silently blame her. Either way, it would poison the relationship."

"I think you're right about that, but I'm sure that doesn't make it any easier."

"It won't be easy," he admitted. "But she's going to be busy the next few days, so maybe a little distance will help. It'll remind me I'm building a life here, but not one that includes Molly."

"Good plan. I've gotta run, Cal, but you should definitely embrace the next few days and use that distance to get your head on straight."

"I will. Thanks, Rome."

By the time Thursday evening rolled around, Callan was very much missing Molly. He'd had a few glimpses of her and they'd bumped into each other at the café, but he hadn't really gotten to talk to her for more than a few minutes.

The time apart wasn't helping.

Now he glanced out his window and when he saw her across the yard, he wasn't even sure it was her for a few seconds. Her hair was restrained in a neat bun, with plain pearl earrings decorating her earlobes and neck. The simple black pantsuit and black flats looked good on her, but as a whole she looked so unlike her usual self he couldn't help watching her for a few minutes.

The mourners were preparing to leave the funeral home, presumably for the cemetery, and she moved among them. She looked so calm and reassuring, it made him smile. Then she slid behind the wheel of the long black car that would follow the hearse Paul was driving, and it made him think about her personal car as he turned away from the window.

She drove a tiny, bright yellow convertible. She wore colorful dresses and sweaters with mermaids on them. She loved to be loud and laugh with the customers at the taproom. She was usually the opposite of the woman he saw helping a family through one of the hardest days of their lives.

It had to be hard for her. The quietness. The restraint. The heavy emotions of the day. No wonder she liked to live the rest of her life out loud.

It was almost time to get ready for bed when he looked out his window for a final time, expecting the windows over the garage to be dark. They were, but what he didn't expect was to see Molly lying in the middle of the yard on a colorful quilt. He was too far away and the streetlight wasn't strong enough for him to see if her eyes were open, but he didn't think even Molly would sleep on a quilt outside. There were way too many bugs for that.

Unable to resist the pull of his curiosity, Callan pulled a lightweight hoodie over his T-shirt and made his way over to her yard. Her eyes weren't closed, so when he was almost to her, she must have caught sight of him in her peripheral vision because she swiveled her head to smile up at him.

"What are you doing out here?" he asked.

"Refilling my happy cup."

"Is that a euphemism for something so overtly personal I shouldn't ask questions about it?"

She chuckled and patted the quilt next to her. He wasn't sure if she was asking him to sit or to lie down next to her, but it was Molly, so he stretched out on his back and looked up at the sky.

"Funerals are hard," she said after a moment. "I feel things in all caps and I also absorb the emotions around me, so I never feel like myself after a funeral. I used to spend days being…well, not depressed in the clinical sense, but very blue, I guess."

"And lying on a quilt helps?" he asked, making sure his voice reflected that he was interested, not judging or mocking.

"It does. Looking up at the night sky and the stars reminds me the world is so much bigger than what I'm feeling in this moment, and the air feels like it's washing away the sorrow. I acknowledge the sadness of the day, but I think about all the moments every funeral has, with little ones playing and then somebody shares a funny story so suddenly it's okay to laugh. And you see that their lives are going to move forward with love and laughter, and I can do the same."

"Helping loved ones mourn is such important work, but I can see how it would be tough emotionally. I'm glad you've found a way to take care of yourself." He watched a drifting cloud heading slowly toward the moon. "Just out of curiosity, what if it's raining?"

She rested her hand on his arm. "If you know me at all, you already know the answer to that."

He chuckled. "You dance."

"Yes, I dance in the rain. If it's raining hard and the yard gets muddy, sometimes I fall and then the next load of laundry sucks, but it's still worth it."

"I can't really picture you holding a funeral event. I saw you earlier, though, from the window. You looked beautiful, though not like yourself."

"I do *not* like the clothes," she said. "And my parents do most of the heavy lifting. But I'm very empathetic and tend to be paying attention to everything all at once, so I'm good at being there with tissues or a chair or a glass of water without anybody having to ask. I help make the service a little easier, so I put up my hair and wear the black suit because that means a lot to me."

All he could think about right now was the warm weight of Molly's hand on his arm. He wanted to roll onto his side so he could pull her close. He wanted to kiss her here on this quilt under the night sky.

But if he did, he wouldn't want to stop. He'd want to kiss her again. And touch her. He definitely wanted to touch her. But getting caught making out in the front yard—of a funeral home, no less—was something this town wouldn't let him live down for a very long time.

"I have a few things to do before I can go to bed, and I should let you get back to refilling your happy cup," he said, rolling away from her so he could push himself to his feet.

He was standing in time to see the flash of disappointment on her face before she gave him a small smile. "My happy cup's pretty full now."

The temptation to read too much into that statement was strong, so he nodded. "I'm glad to hear it. Good night, Molly."

Walking away from her lying on that quilt without looking back was incredibly hard, but Callan forced himself to do it. If he looked back and she was watching him, he'd go back. And he'd used up all his willpower getting this far, so if he went back he'd end up spending the night with her and even though they'd been in his bed or hers several times, he was still reeling from her revelation.

In two days, the town would gather to celebrate Old Home Day and they'd already decided they'd stage their breakup shortly after. He could only hope that would be enough time for him to figure out what he was going to do.

He couldn't imagine the rest of his life without Molly in it. But now he couldn't imagine his life *with* her, either.

Chapter Sixteen

*Happy Old Home Day! The parade departs
from the school parking lot at ten o'clock and
will go through town and around the square
before returning to the school. The sidewalk
sales and vendors on the square will go until
five o'clock, and the annual used book sale is
happening on the library lawn, so hydrate and
don't forget your sunscreen!*
—Stonefield Gazette *Facebook Page*

Molly loved Old Home Day. It was an entire day
to celebrate community and life in a small town,
and there was so much to do. The parade. Booths.
Games. Food. The used book sale. And not once in

the entire history of Cyrs Funeral Home had they had to host a service on Old Home Day.

"Did you just knock on that tree?" Callan asked in a voice heavy with amusement.

"Yeah. I had a thought and then I was afraid I was going to jinx something, so I had to knock on wood. Trees are wood."

"What was the thought?"

She gave him some serious side-eye. "Obviously I can't tell you or I'll have to knock on another tree and the bark is really hard on my knuckles."

"Where are we going, anyway?"

"To find a good spot to watch the parade. We want to be able to see everything, but also be close enough to the library so you can get there by the time the parade disperses. The book sale early birds don't mess around, you know."

She also wanted a place that was free of Suttons, Danforths and Thompsons, though she didn't tell him that. She wanted him all to herself today, as much as possible, because there weren't going to be too many more days she could call herself Callan's girlfriend.

"While I like the fact that *book sale early birds* exist," Callan was saying, "I don't think the situation's that urgent."

Not five minutes after the parade turned the final corner back to the school, Callan got a call from a guy on the library committee because there were two women waiting to buy a pile of books and they couldn't find him.

"Okay, I guess it's urgent," he admitted. "I hate to abandon you already."

"I'll wander over in a little while, after I've gotten snacks and made sure I'm not missing any *big* sidewalk sale bargains."

He put his hand on her hip, pulling her closer. "Are you going to bring me snacks?"

"I might." She could feel the smile curving his lips when he kissed her. "I'll see you soon."

She watched him walk away until he was out of sight, admiring the way his butt looked in those pants. Then she turned to go in search of kettle corn and almost walked into Mallory and Evie. When she jumped back, a guilty flush making her face hot, they both gave her knowing looks.

"You never responded to the text I sent you after Gwen's reception," Evie said.

"That was like two weeks ago, and I get so many I don't even know if I saw it. What did it say?"

"It said not to have sex with Callan."

"Oh." Molly felt a guilty flush spreading across her cheeks. "I did see that one."

"When?"

"Right after I had sex with Callan."

"Molly!" Mallory winced and looked around to see if anybody was looking at them before lowering her voice. "That was a bad idea."

"Nope. It was one of my better ideas. Trust me."

"So that's why you've been avoiding us?" Evie demanded. "Because you didn't want to hear us praising your great idea?"

"Avoiding you? I was there for Books & Brews, and for comedy night."

"You're usually around a *lot* more," Mallory said.

"I've been busy. I don't actually work for Sutton's Place, you know." She crossed her arms, hoping she looked defiant, but Evie rolled her eyes and Mallory shook her head. "Okay, fine. It wasn't a great idea. It was a great *night* but I shouldn't have done it."

"But you've done it again, right?" Mallory asked.

She nodded. "Several times. We're next-door neighbors and it's so…easy to visit each other."

Evie looked confused. "So it's a real thing now?"

"No. We're still fake dating. It's just fun on the side, I guess." And that was all it could be, since she'd seen his face when she told him she wasn't having kids. Unless he wasn't as invested in having children as he said he was, there was no chance their relationship was going anywhere real.

"Okay, let's go find some kettle corn," Mallory said, and that cheered Molly up. "I probably won't have long before Irish leaves the brewery's booth and comes looking for me to make sure I'm not overdoing it."

Wandering around the square with Mallory and Evie brightened Molly's spirits considerably. Gwen joined them after a while, with her dog, Boomer, at her side. Molly knelt down to give his neck proper scratching and she laughed when he licked her cheek.

It was almost like old times for a little bit. But then Evie had to go back to Sutton's Seconds because Becca needed to get home and it wasn't fair for Laura to have to leave. And when Irish caught up with Mallory and invited her to sit in the shade with him for a while, Gwen and Boomer went to join Case and Lane at the taproom's booth.

She was making a game plan for snacks when she turned a corner and almost ran into her parents. Cyrs Funeral Home didn't have a booth, of course, because nobody wanted that, so they were free to enjoy the festivities.

"Enjoying yourself, honey?" her father asked.

"I am. I'm going to go help Callan with the used book sale, but I'm going to get some snacks for us first." When her mother's face pinched slightly, she frowned because she couldn't figure out what she'd said wrong. "He's not going to leave the book sale, Mom. I'm bringing the snacks to him."

"What?" Amanda shook her head, clearly confused. "I didn't say anything about the snacks, Molly."

"You gave me a disapproval face."

"You're so dramatic, Molly. And that's what I'm worried about."

So she was right. She'd done something to displease her mother without even trying and without even knowing what it was. "What *are* you worried about?"

"You're just a lot and I hope if you get to be too much for Callan, he doesn't run back to the city. He's doing wonders with the library and it's not just that the library committee doesn't want to go through the whole search again. I really think he's the best man for the job. And your ex-boyfriends have a tendency to leave town."

Molly was so angry she laughed. It was weird, but she couldn't help it. "Cory left for college and Hunter got a job offer in Boston. I'm not driving men out of Stonefield, Mom. And by the way, Hunter was a real jerk."

"Dial it back, honey," her dad said in a soft voice. "We don't want to be the family that has a huge argument in the middle of Old Home Day."

"Oh no. Maybe I'll start a mass exodus of people fleeing our town to get away from us."

"Molly!" Amanda sighed and shook her head. "Forget I said anything."

But she couldn't forget. As she walked through the crowd, grabbing some food you could only get at fairs and celebrations like this, she couldn't shake the idea that her mother would be Team Callan in their impending breakup. The town's librarian was more important to Amanda than her own daughter.

She recognized on some level that she was overreacting slightly. Her mother, as one of the people who'd chosen Callan to be their librarian, was concerned that a breakup between him and her daughter could make things awkward for everybody.

But it was the assumption that a breakup was inevitable because Molly was *too much* that had her unable to calm herself down. Her own mother thought she was going to blow up her relationship to the point Callan might run away just by being herself.

Callan was used to the jolt of happiness and anticipation he always got when he saw Molly coming toward him, but it fizzled out fairly quickly when he realized something was going on with her.

She smiled and she had snacks. But the smile was forced and she didn't give him a fast, animated rundown of why she'd chosen each of the foods she had and a recap of everybody she'd run into. She just put the snacks on the library steps so he could help himself and went to straighten some books on the cookbook blanket. He'd just straightened those, though, spreading them out to hide the fact they were as low on cookbook inventory as they were on mysteries. That blanket was almost empty already.

Molly wasn't being Molly.

Something had happened to upset her. He could see her tension in the rigidity of her spine and the way she held her shoulders. She was stewing in anxiety and frustration and one of the things he'd seen online is that somebody wired the way Molly was might not be able to calm down—she wasn't necessarily self-soothing—and she might need a way to distract her brain away from the issue it was hung up on.

It wasn't his place to intercede. He was neither a therapist nor her actual boyfriend, but he hated to see her like this. "Hey Molly, what's your favorite color?"

Her head whipped around, her face blank for a few seconds before it brightened. "Pink. No. Purple. But also yellow?"

"Is teal blue or green?"

She laughed. "It's both. Isn't it?"

He shrugged. "I don't know."

"You're not going to paint your walls teal, are you?" She bounced on her toes, and he knew if he was closer, she would have slapped his arm. His Molly was coming back. "Oh, I should paint my mom's office teal while she's out of the house."

"I don't know if she'd like that."

"I don't care if she doesn't like it. She thinks my personality will make you flee Stonefield and she'll have to find another librarian and she doesn't want to because you're so awesome at it."

And there it was—an argument with Amanda. His professional ego could feast on the compliment from a library committee later. For now he needed to figure out how to navigate Molly's emotions when they stemmed from conflict with her mother.

He could remind her that it was a nonissue because they already had a plan for breaking up and it didn't involve him leaving his job and his half-renovated house behind. There was no sense in being angry about something that wasn't going to happen.

But it wasn't that. Her mother just assumed she was going to end up alone because Callan would get sick of the quirks that came with Molly's ADHD. That had to be painful for her, since it was coming from the woman who should know and love her more than anybody else.

Keeping his mouth shut was probably his best option.

"They have deep-fried candy bars this year," she said. "I've never had one, but I want to. I was going to get one for us, but I was afraid it would be gross by the time I got it here. So later I'm going to ask Laura to cover for a few minutes so we can go get one."

So a conversational U-turn back to snacks, he thought, smiling. At least she'd shaken off the awful tension and had fully embraced the anticipation of trying what sounded to him like a disgusting food choice. He'd try it, though, and he might even pretend to like it because her joy over trying a new fair food for the first time was infectious. And because it had completed the mission of distracting her from the darker emotions that had been weighing her down.

After giving him a bright smile that proved him right, she turned her attention to a woman who was trying to juggle an armful of paperbacks she'd chosen. "Mrs. Cloutier, did you know the Stonefield Library tote bags are only five dollars today?"

He watched her interacting with people while he ate a handful of kettle corn. The last couple of days hadn't been easy, and keeping a smile on his face today was quite a challenge. But he was determined not to let her know their talk about kids had changed anything between them because he didn't want her to feel as if she was responsible for breaking his heart.

If Callan had his way, Roman was going to be the only person in their circle of friends who knew he wasn't just a guy upholding the terms of their original agreement—once Old Home Day was over, it was time to break up.

Chapter Seventeen

*We've had a lot of people asking in the com-
ments about the mystery business going in next
door to the Perkin' Up Café, where Barton Insurance used to be. We don't have the answer,
but we've asked around and it seems to be the
best-kept secret in Stonefield! We even went
to town hall because somebody there has to
know, but nobody's talking!*
     —Stonefield Gazette *Facebook Page*

When he'd started weeding out the books that
should no longer be in the collection—either due to
physical condition or being *extremely* outdated—
Callan hadn't considered he would be left with the

significant problem of how to fill the gaps on the shelves.

He'd known there would be some bare spots. Just with a cursory glance, he'd been able to tell the parenting section would be decimated. One of the books still suggested the safest place for a baby to ride was in a basket on the floor behind the driver's seat. That particular book he was going to put in one of the glass cases that held books that were too interesting to discard, but couldn't be checked out and wouldn't be used for educational purposes. But the rest of them were almost as bad.

Computers. Business. Automotive. Almost every section needed weeding as badly as a garden gone untended for decades. And he knew, of course, that library research had become less of a thing with the rise of the internet. Why go to the library and pore through weighty books when you could ask your phone and get the answer without leaving your chair? That didn't mean he was going to settle for shelves of dusty, obsolete books.

But he could condense the nonfiction to make room for the three projects that were highest on his list. He wanted to replace the old computer shoved in a corner with an updated computer station with at least three desktops and a central printer. The transition to doing things online, even in public schools, assumed socioeconomic privilege, and he wanted to ensure no resident of Stonefield went without access to the internet.

He wanted to establish a YA space. The collection currently transitioned from the children's section to adult, and he wanted teens to have a space of their own. It couldn't be very big, but print books had seen a resurgence with the age group that lived their lives online, and they needed more shelf space and some comfortable seating. Maybe some art from the high school art classes, which he'd have to look into.

Finally, the fiction. Mrs. Denning had developed an impressive collection and the circulation numbers told him she'd chosen well. Obviously she knew what the residents of Stonefield liked to read, and his job was to keep supplying them with the books they wanted. But there was a lack of diversity in the catalog, and he intended to work on that.

His phone vibrated in his pocket, startling him. Rome wouldn't try to video chat with him during library hours. He was good about that.

When he pulled the phone out and saw a text message from Molly, he smiled. The smile faded quickly, though, because she knew he was working and while she might stop in and talk to him, she never texted him during library hours.

Unless it was an emergency.

Then the phone registered his face and unlocked the preview. Mallory's in labor!

He couldn't tell if the exclamation point was one

of excitement or panic, but he typed in the first thing that popped into head.

Does she need a ride to the hospital?

No, Irish is taking her and Ellen. I just thought you'd want to know!

Callan assumed that meant he wasn't expected to rush to the hospital along with the rest of them. Best wishes to her and the baby. I hope they're both healthy and happy.

I'll let you know when the baby's born. THIS IS SO EXCITING!

Excitement was definitely better than panic, he thought as he slid the phone back into his pocket. But he couldn't stop thinking about the situation when he tried to go back to what he was doing.

Was there an expectation a guy would do something for the birth of his girlfriend's best friend's baby? Flowers, maybe? He couldn't possibly be expected to go to the hospital and wait with Molly. Could he?

He'd go pull an etiquette book off the shelf, but the last one he'd flipped through had suggested a woman should put on a clean dress and touch up her hair and makeup five minutes before her husband was due to return from work, so he wasn't sure how helpful that would be in the current century.

By the time thirty minutes had passed, he couldn't stand it anymore. Molly's best friend was having a baby, so she'd be excited and worried and everything would be heightened for her. He should be with her. At the very least he could bring her a charging cord for her phone because she never had one and there was no way of knowing how long she'd be at the hospital.

He knew her friends and family group well enough to know they'd all gather, and he wanted to be a part of that. He'd come to care for them a lot, and if Mallory was in labor for a long time, maybe he could be useful to them. He could make coffee runs or pick up food.

But mostly he wanted to be there to hold Molly's hand.

Molly shouldn't have sent that text to Callan. It had been an impulse—to share the exciting news with him—and it wasn't until she was sitting in the waiting room with the Sutton family that she'd realized it was an impulse she should have put the brakes on.

He wasn't *really* her boyfriend. But she had no brakes when it came to impulses, so she'd interrupted him at work to share news that probably meant nothing to him.

"Are you okay, Molly?" It was Evie who asked,

her brows drawn in concern. "You look angry, which is really unlike you."

"I'm okay." She fixed her face into a happy smile. "Just replaying a conversation in my head."

"I hope it's not from middle school this time." Evie shook her head, chuckling. "You're always doing that—reliving something from the past and feeling some kind of way about it all over again. I remember when Brad Dupont came to visit his parents and stopped by the taproom and after he left, you were almost in tears because you said something mean to him in sixth grade."

"I still feel bad about it," Molly said, feeling the familiar guilt at having pointed out Brad's rather nasty pimple right before he had to stand up in front of the class to read a paper. She hadn't intended to be mean—she wasn't sure if he knew that touching it so much would make it worse—but he'd been flustered when the teacher called his name.

It was just a curse she lived with—the ability to remember and relive every embarrassment or bad moment of her entire life. Usually when she was trying to sleep and something triggered a memory she'd rather forget. There was nothing like insomnia fueled by thinking a person you'd only met one time ten years ago might think badly of you because something you'd said had come out wrong.

"Who was the conversation with?" Evie asked, and she must have noticed Molly's quick glance toward Ellen and Laura in the corner. "Come on. Who knows how long we'll be here and I'm child-free. Let's go scope out the vending machines."

Once they were out of earshot of the others, Evie nudged her. "Tell me. I assume, since you didn't want to say in front of Mom and Laura, that it has to do with your *boyfriend*."

"I sent him a text telling him Mallory's in labor," she admitted.

"And?"

"And he said best wishes and all that, and to let him know when the baby's born."

"Okay, so why does thinking about that have you tied up in mental knots?"

Molly wasn't sure she could explain it. "Because it's the kind of text you send to your boyfriend."

"Which he's supposed to be, as far as everybody knows."

"But *we* know he's not. So if somebody was watching or if it was a phone call I made in front of our people, that would be one thing. But nobody's reading our text messages."

"Molly, you are really overthinking this, as per usual." She said it with affection, though, so the words didn't cut the way they did when her mother said them. "Even though it kind of happened because of the whole fake dating thing, Callan has built relationships with all of us. He's a friend. He was at

Gwen's wedding. Not only is it totally normal that you texted him the news, but I'm sure he *wants* to know."

"Okay, that's good, but if you're all friends, what's going to happen when we break up?"

"Your brain really doesn't like to take the win, does it. On to the next worry." Evie shook her head. "Look, to be honest, none of us think that's actually going to happen."

Molly didn't understand. "What do you mean?"

"Just what I said. None of us think that breakup is going to happen."

"It is," she argued in as firm a tone as she could muster. She didn't want to explain the reason why while they were standing around at a vending machine, but they were all wrong.

"Then you two should get on the first bus to Hollywood because your acting skills would win you all the awards."

"Okay, so the attraction isn't fake. Our friendship isn't fake. The sex is certainly real. He is literally everything I could want in a husband except for one thing. He wants children. Plural. I'm not having any."

Evie sighed and dropped her head. The Sutton sisters had all made their opinions on that choice clear over the years, and they didn't agree with her decision at all. They'd given up trying to change her mind a long time ago, though.

"I'd say if it's meant to be, you can work through anything," Evie said. "But that's a big one, I guess."

"Yeah." She was going to say more, but then she heard Callan's voice and froze. "He's here."

"Of course he's here. He knows you're here waiting and he's going to keep you company. No matter what mess you two have gotten yourselves into, he's a good guy and he's your friend. Stop overanalyzing things and go see him. I'm getting a candy bar, but I'll be along."

When Molly turned the corner back to the waiting room, Callan was with everybody else who'd shown up to wait. Almost everybody was there, though Laura and Lane had stayed home with Becca so Evie could come, and they also had Jack and Eli.

Callan was holding a small brown teddy bear, obviously from the gift shop, and her heart squeezed painfully as Evie's words echoed through her mind.

He's a good guy and he's your friend.

He was the *best* guy, and she hugged him fiercely. "You didn't have to come. We have no idea how long it'll take."

She'd barely gotten the words out before Irish appeared at the other end of the waiting room. His eyes were damp, but he was grinning as everybody stood and turned toward him.

"We have a daughter," he said, his voice thick with emotion. "I've got a little baby girl and her name is Leeza. Mallory's fine and Ellen's with her while they finish up, and they didn't want me to bring the baby out here, but I held her and I've got a picture here."

They all gathered around his phone and Molly was aware of Callan's arm around her waist as they all took turns peering at the tiny little face on the screen. They all agreed she was perfect, and Irish had to clear his throat twice before he could speak.

"I'm going to call the boys, but can somebody send this to Laura so they can see her?" He wasn't great with technology, though he was getting better. "She's going to bring them over later, but I want them to see her now."

It was almost an hour before it was Molly's turn to see Mallory, and she turned to Callan, but he shook his head. "You go ahead. Tell her I said congratulations and give her this from us. And I'll see the baby once they've had a chance to settle in at home."

She only had ten minutes with Mallory and Leeza before Laura arrived with Jack and Eli. Big brothers took precedence over aunts, so Molly kissed Leeza's head and Mallory's cheek before making her way back to the waiting room.

It wasn't until she and Callan were leaving that she realized it was late afternoon, but not *that* early.

"Did you close the library?"

He chuckled. "I thought that was a better idea than putting a note on the door asking patrons to check out their own books. The date stamp is so fun to play with, they might never leave."

"Today was a lot," she said, and that was an understatement. "Want to grab a pizza and hang out at my place tonight?"

He opened her car door for her, stepping back so she could get in. "Sounds good. I have to run back to the library and close it up properly, so if you call in the pizza for about an hour from now, I can pick it up on my way."

When she nodded, he leaned in and kissed her before closing her door. It was sweet, and she was smiling as she backed out of her parking spot and pointed her car toward home.

Chapter Eighteen

There's a new cowgirl in town! Irish and Mallory Sutton welcomed a baby girl into the world, and Grandma Ellen reports both mother and daughter are healthy and happy. She wouldn't tell us the baby's name, but if you stop by the taproom and congratulate the new dad, our resident cowboy just might tell you! Congratulations, Sutton Family!

—Stonefield Gazette *Facebook Page*

Something had changed in Callan since Mallory'd had her baby. She'd seen a look on his face when they were in the hospital that she'd seen before—when she was holding Becca at the wedding breakfast.

Becca and Leeza were very real and visible reminders of the thing Callan wanted most, and that Molly wouldn't give him. And she knew the clock had started ticking in earnest on their couple charade. But one of her most useful, if also most self-sabotaging, skills was her ability to put something out of her mind to think about another day. Usually that *another day* didn't come until whatever the unpleasant thing was became a crisis. If she really thought about it, she knew better, but it often happened on a subconscious level.

She'd been shoving thoughts of her impending heartbreak down as much as possible, but Leeza's birth seemed to have driven the truth of their situation home, and Callan wasn't hiding it well.

"You're very quiet tonight," she said, stroking his hair in that way that made him purr. They were on his couch in the living room that was finally finished, including the new furniture that had finally been delivered.

"Sorry. I'm a little tired and I was just lost in thought, I guess. Not any particular thoughts, I guess, other than it's nice to have my living room put back together and a couch made in this century."

Molly was pretty sure he wasn't being totally honest with her. He might have spared a thought or two about his living room, but he had something much more serious on his mind. But because she was afraid she knew what it might be and that kicked her into avoidance mode, she didn't call him on it.

Instead, she stroked his hair and tried to pay attention to the show they were watching. It was some FBI series or something he'd been watching for years and she'd gladly offered to watch it with him, though she had no idea what was happening. But she tried to follow it just to give her mind something to do other than obsessing about Callan's thoughts.

She didn't have to wonder about where his thoughts had roamed to when the hand that was resting on her thigh started making slow circles heading north. And she had to admit she found it flattering when he pulled her into his arms for a thorough kiss.

When he led her into the almost finished bedroom, Molly managed to forget her concerns for a little while. Callan's hands and mouth were very good at distracting her, and he certainly knew how to make good use of them.

But there was something different between them even in bed. There was a shadow in his expression when he gazed into her eyes. His touch lingered, as though he was memorizing her body. She wasn't sure what any of it meant, but she had to reach between their bodies and stroke herself in order to find release.

When Callan's orgasm had passed, he collapsed on top of her, but instead of burying his face in her hair as he often did, he pressed kisses to her cheek and her jaw before kissing her shoulder.

Minutes later, when she tried to slide out of bed, he stirred. "Are you staying tonight?"

She did sometimes, but she didn't want to tonight. The vibe was off in ways she couldn't quite nail down and she would never go to sleep. She'd lie awake all night, replaying every word and every look, trying to find the key to the change in his mood and trying to find a way to get back what they'd had.

"I can't. I have an early morning, so I need to take care of a few things tonight. But maybe we'll do coffee."

"I'll text you," he mumbled, almost asleep again.

After putting her clothes back on—as tempting as it was to just sprint the very short distance to her door and hope for the best—she turned off his lights and locked his door behind her.

If she was going to lie awake wondering what was going on with Callan, at least she could do it in her own bed so *he* could get some sleep.

For the first time in their friendship, Callan wasn't in the mood to answer Rome's call. He was too busy feeling sorry for himself, and his best friend was way too perceptive. He'd end up having to talk about his feelings and he didn't want to do that. It was painful enough without speaking the words.

But wallowing wasn't good for him, so he hit the button and actually felt his spirits lift when Rome's face filled the screen.

"Callan, what the hell? You look like shit."

Well, that didn't last long. "Thanks, Rome."

"What's going on? You don't have the flu or something, do you?"

He really looked *that* bad? "No, I'm not sick. I didn't get enough sleep last night. That's all."

"For all the right reasons?"

"Not really, no." Resigned to talking about it, he leaned back in his chair with a heavy sigh. "I let it go too far."

"The fake dating's not going well?"

"It's going too well. That's the problem. It sure as hell isn't going to feel fake when I tell her it's over."

"And that's where you are?"

"I think so. I mean, everything at the library is better than I could have imagined. I'm not nervous about my job or my place in the community anymore, which means every day we continue the charade, it's simply because we *want* to and it becomes less of a charade."

Rome nodded his understanding. "What's going to happen when you stage your breakup?"

"People have gotten to know me and everybody seems comfortable with me in the library. I don't think it's going to be a problem anymore."

"But if everybody loves Molly so much, won't you become the villain of the story?"

Callan snorted. "Couples break up. It's a thing

that happens and very rarely does anybody get run out of town on a rail."

"You got into this mess because you were worried about that town's perception of you, but now you seem pretty cavalier about it."

"As I said, they've gotten to know me now, and that was the whole point. Plus we're past the probationary period, so I feel a lot more secure about my job."

"It would be one thing if it was a couple of weeks. You go on a few dates. People see you with her. Still ridiculous, but I can see that."

"The whole idea was that I be in a *committed* relationship," Callan reminded him.

"Exactly. You've been in this so-called *committed* relationship for almost two months, plus however long you were supposed to have been talking online. You're a couple to all of them, and the longer you go on thinking so, the more they have expectations you two are the real deal. And the breakup will be that much of a bigger deal." Rome leaned back in his chair and shook his head. "And then you'll be the villain and single and ready to find a new woman, which brings you right back to where you started."

Tough love was one thing, but Rome was really starting to annoy him. "I won't be back where I started. I've gotten the chance to show them I'm a good guy, and a big part of it will be that they won't have to rally around Molly because she won't be heartbroken and moping around Stonefield. Now some guy's wife going into the library where I'm working won't be any different than going into the market or the hardware store or anywhere else a guy's working."

"Okay." It was clear from Rome's expression he didn't totally buy it, but he wasn't going to get anywhere.

"And what if we don't?" Callan asked before he thought about whether or not he should say the words aloud.

Rome tilted his head. "What if you don't *what*?"

"Break up."

"Callan. Dude. I swear if I wasn't flying to Japan the day after tomorrow, I'd get in my car and head to New Hampshire right now. What are you doing?"

Callan swallowed hard past the lump in his throat. "I told you it's not fake anymore, Rome, and I meant it. It hasn't been for a long time. I'm madly in love with Molly."

To his friend's credit, he didn't react right away. Rome thought about it for a few moments, but when the lines of his face softened, Callan knew he didn't really want to hear what Rome had to say.

"There's a part of me that's so happy for you, Callan. I want nothing but happiness for you, and she clearly makes you happy. But you already know— since *you* are the one who told me—that the happiness won't last. You're the one who said not having kids would eventually poison your relationship with her and you're not wrong, no matter how much you want to be."

"I don't want to give her up." There would be an emptiness in his life where she should be, and he couldn't imagine anybody else ever filling that space.

"Then you give up on having kids."

Callan scrubbed his hands over his face. "A family's all I've ever wanted. I can't."

"Then it's time," Rome said gently. "And it has nothing to do with people's expectations. The longer you let this go on, the worse that pain you're feeling right now is going to get."

Chapter Nineteen

A reminder from the Stonefield Library: in addition to books, audiobooks, videos, programs and much more, did you know you can sign out day passes for some of New Hampshire's most popular attractions, from science museums to the planetarium? Stop by or visit their website for more information!
—Stonefield Gazette *Facebook Page*

Molly was happy it was a Monday because it meant the taproom was closed and she could just face-plant on her bed if she wanted to, even though it wasn't even supper time yet. She'd helped out all weekend so Irish could keep going into the house to check on Mallory and the baby, and they'd been busier than usual because everybody wanted to congratulate Irish and see pictures of Leeza.

Plus her parents had decided the trim needed repainting in all of the public rooms. Especially the bottom trim because it got scuffed by chair legs being moved around. That had required a lot of plastic sheeting and since she was the young one, she got to do the crouching down part of the painting.

No matter how tired she was though, she seemed to have some kind of internal alarm that let her know when it was library closing time. And when she heard Callan's footsteps on the stairs, she smiled. He was about to knock on the door at the top of the staircase when she opened it.

"Hey, come on in," she said, taking a step back. She expected a hello kiss as he went by, but he looked distracted and didn't pause.

He went straight to her couch and sat down on the edge, looking stiff and uncomfortable. Then he looked up at her briefly and she'd never seen his face so serious. "We need to talk about this dating thing."

"What do you mean?"

He picked at an imaginary fuzz on his pants, then, not meeting her eyes. "I think it's time to end the ruse."

Panic swept through Molly, making her skin tingle, but she tried to force it back. Maybe he meant that it was time to stop pretending there was a ruse at all—to admit that somewhere along the way, it had all become real. And that he was okay with not having kids because she was worth it.

"I think Stonefield's gotten to know me well enough," he continued. "But when two people date for a length of time, people start expecting...things."

He paused, as though to give her an opportunity to speak, but she couldn't come up with anything to say. There were too many emotions clamoring around in her head to form any kind of a coherent thought.

"I want us to still be friends," he continued, as if she and millions of other women hadn't heard *that* before. "I mean it, Molly. I don't want to lose what we have, but we have to stop pretending it's something it's not before—"

"I get it," she said, cutting him off because she didn't want to hear anymore. It was taking every bit of focus and self-discipline she could fight for to keep her expression neutral and her eyes dry. The longer he was in this room talking, the harder it was going to get. "It's time."

He stood and there was a long, awkward moment when it looked like he might be deciding on whether or not to hug her. If he did, she'd have a complete and total breakdown, so she took a step back.

"I was just on my way out," she lied. "But of course we'll still be friends. I'll probably see you at the café tomorrow."

"Okay." He shoved his hands in his pockets and

his shoulders rose and fell as he took a deep breath. "I'll... I guess I'll see you tomorrow."

As soon as her door closed behind him, Molly wanted to collapse into a heap of sobbing misery, but she refused to allow herself to do that. She'd gotten herself into this situation and, just as her friends had warned her would happen, she'd put her whole heart into it.

Now it was broken and she had nobody to blame but herself.

Without thinking it through—just wanting him to leave—she'd told him she was on her way out, so now she had to go somewhere. She didn't want to, but it probably beat crying all night, even if all she did was drive around in circles.

She ended up at the Sutton house because that was where she always went when she was looking for comfort. And she needed her best friend.

Luckily, Ellen was out and Irish had taken the boys fishing, so she had Mallory to herself. And Leeza, of course.

Mallory had taken one look at Molly and settled into the rocking chair with the baby in her arms. "Tell me everything. But promise me you won't be offended if I fall asleep while you're talking to me."

"It's me, Mal. There's a good chance I won't even notice."

"That's true. What happened?"

"It was nothing dramatic. I guess he decided it

was time for the act to come to an end. We agreed to fake date for a reason and it worked. It was the plan all along for us to break up at some point." She shrugged as if she could force herself to believe it meant that little. "I guess we reached that point."

"I didn't even realize you two were still *fake* dating. I honestly thought it just became a real thing along the way. We all did."

"We never talked about it but, to be honest, I think I felt that way, too. I just never thought about it, I guess. We were just together and I enjoyed it and the labels didn't really matter to me."

"But he wasn't faking, either. I've seen you together too often not to see that, and I don't understand what happened."

"Yes, you do. You even warned me, remember? The picket fence?" Molly flopped back against the chair with a sigh. "He wants kids more than he wants me."

"Molly, I don't think it's that cut-and-dried, and you know that sometimes you read more into things than what's really there. Does he know how you feel?"

"He knows I don't want to have kids."

"Did you tell him why? And I actually meant, does he know that you weren't faking anymore, not how you feel about kids."

"I told him why I can't have kids, and he didn't

push like you guys, but I don't think he really understands."

"Of course he doesn't." Mallory shifted the baby on her shoulder, trying to get comfortable. "Try to imagine your parents not wanting children because they might have *you*. And don't even tell me they probably would have been happier that way because you know that's the chemicals in your brain lying to you. You're amazing and we all love you so much, so hearing you say you're afraid to make a little person who's like you doesn't make sense to those of us who love you and wouldn't change a single thing about you."

"It was so hard, though. It still is."

"I don't know what it's like to be in your head, but I know what it's been like to be your best friend for your entire life. I can see that it's hard for you sometimes, but I can also see that you went all through childhood and school with no idea *why* it was hard. And a lot of the people in your life still don't give you the support and grace they should."

"Callan does," she said without thinking. "He researched ADHD and he's learned about things that are hard for me and he adapts how we do things so it works for me. He doesn't make me choose things and he knows how to distract me when I can't calm down and he lets me talk through movies."

"Molly, that man loves you."

"He wants us to be friends."

"He probably wants more than that. He wants to stop pretending because he wants it to be real, but you both know it won't work out in the long run if you can't agree on children, so what else is he supposed to do?"

"I don't know. I wish… I just wish things could have kept going the way they were."

"Which would have gotten you what *you* wanted—him and only him. But he still wouldn't have gotten what he wanted."

"I want him to be happy," Molly said because it was the truth. Then she swiped at a tear running down her cheek. "But I want me to be happy, too."

When Callan woke the next morning, he told himself going to the Perkin' Up Café would be a bad idea. He repeated it to the steamy mirror after his shower. He chanted it like a mantra as he walked down the sidewalk.

And he said it out loud as he pulled open the café's door and stepped inside.

He wanted to see Molly. He *needed* to see her, actually. Maybe if he could see her now, not long after her alarm went off, he'd know the truth. If she was her usual bright-eyed, cheerful self, he would know he'd never been more than a fake boyfriend and a no-strings fling.

But if he could see the evidence of a sleepless night and maybe some tears, he'd know it had been more to her. Maybe that was worse. Maybe knowing she cared for him would make it harder, but he didn't think so. He'd find some solace in that, even though it wouldn't change anything.

His gaze sought her out as though he had some kind of inner Molly radar. She was leaning against the counter, talking to Chelsea, but she stopped when he walked in. It seemed to take forever to reach the counter, as if he was moving in slow motion, and he kept reminding himself that technically nothing had changed. If the dating hadn't been real, the breakup couldn't be real. And she'd agreed they'd still be friends, so there was no reason to avoid her.

"Good morning, ladies," he said, trying to sound as natural as possible. It didn't come out any more natural than the forced smiles they gave him in return.

Molly clearly hadn't slept well. He wouldn't say it made him happy, but it gave him a little peace of mind. If she'd cried, it had either been only a few tears or she had an exceptional way with makeup. Her eyes were slightly red, but not puffy at all.

What didn't make him happy was that she'd lost her sparkle. Not totally, but it had definitely been dimmed. Sure, it was temporary and it let him know their relationship hadn't meant nothing to her, but he didn't want her to be hurting as much as he was.

"The usual?" Chelsea asked.

"Yes, please." She stepped away to prepare his

coffee, her back to him, and he really hoped she wouldn't mess up his drink on purpose to get back at him for breaking up with her friend. A shot of hazelnut flavoring wasn't going to improve his day at all.

"Have you ordered the next Books & Brews books from interlibrary loan yet?" she asked, and he could see she was trying like hell for a light, breezy tone. She missed, but the effort gave him hope they could maybe come out of this with their friendship intact.

"Not yet. I found the movie on a streaming service, though. I already read the book, so I'll watch it.

Her laugh was like a balm to his ragged nerves. "I don't know if I'll read the book. But the movie's in my notebook with a star next to it, so I'll watch it in time.

"Here you go," Chelsea said. "I'll add it to your tab."

"Thank you." He couldn't very well take the lid off and sniff it for errant flavorings right in front of her, so he'd have to take his chances. After picking up the cup, he smiled at Molly. "I'll see you around, I guess."

"You live next door, so probably," she said, and her return smile didn't reach her eyes. "Have a good day at work, Callan."

There was nothing he could really say to that since he already knew he wasn't going to have a good today. Tomorrow didn't look good, either. He wasn't sure how long it would take for him get through a day without thoughts of Molly filling him with heart-break and regret, but it wouldn't be anytime soon.

He nodded and forced himself to turn around and walk out of the café without looking back.

Molly managed to hold the frustration and pain in check until the door closed behind Callan, but as soon as he was gone, she made a sound like a toddler having a temper tantrum. She couldn't help it, and she was thankful the only customers in the place had left about two minutes before her ex-fake-boyfriend walked in.

"I'm super proud of you for not doing that while he was still here," Chelsea said, shaking her head. "I know that was hard for you."

"I meant to get my drink and run so I'd be gone before he got here, but then we started talking and I waited too long."

"If it's any consolation, he looks as unhappy as you do."

Molly sighed. "It's not really a consolation. It's a reminder that we're probably actually meant to be together, but I can't ask him to give up his dream of having kids. And I can't get past my fear of having kids who'll be miserable."

"For what it's worth, Molly, I think you'd be a great mom. You don't have to be perfect, you know. No moms are. You would love your kid the way you do everything—with your whole heart and so much love and joy."

"But no clean laundry and a lost field trip permission slip and missing homework assignments I should have followed up on and didn't."

"Molly Cyrs, are you wearing dirty underwear right now?"

She actually gasped. "No. I am *not*, thank you very much."

"So why would your kid? You make it sound like you can't do anything, and you actually can. I know you have to work a little harder at it and have your notebook and all but you're so awesome at so many things. And so many people love you."

Molly wished she could find the right words to make everybody understand her fear that a child of hers would be unhappy. And it would be her fault. Molly's ADHD didn't seem to have come from either of her parents, but if it had, wouldn't she blame that parent?

Or maybe she wouldn't have had such a hard time growing up because the parent with ADHD would have understood her and supported her.

"Tell me something," Chelsea said, in that tone friends use to indicate they're about to throw down a winning hand. "Why can't your kid have a notebook?"

Chapter Twenty

*We spotted a help-wanted ad you (or a friend)
might be interested in. D&T Tree Service is
looking to hire an experienced foreman and
we can vouch for their business practices and
great customer service. If you or somebody you
know is interested, contact Laura Thompson!*
—Stonefield Gazette *Facebook Page*

Callan didn't want to unlock the library doors this
morning. Usually it was one of his favorite parts of
the day, but his heart wasn't in it. Not today, when
that heart was broken.

Another restless night thinking about Molly. Another day of his first waking thought being regret.
At least today he'd been smart enough to skip the

café. Lack of sleep and thirty-six hours or so of her not being his fake girlfriend had weakened him to the point he was afraid if he saw her, he'd drop to his knees and beg her to take him back—for real this time—and to hell with his hopes and dreams.

Instead, he'd filled a travel mug at home and left his house earlier than usual. It took a lot of restraint not to look up at the window over the garage as he walked past, and he made it to the library without running into anybody who wanted to stop and talk.

But judging by how fast the news he was Molly's boyfriend had spread through Stonefield, he knew there was a good chance some of the patrons who walked through the door today were going to know he *wasn't* her boyfriend anymore. The last thing he wanted to do was talk about their "breakup" because maybe his mind knew there were quotation marks around that word, but his heart didn't.

He'd messed up. It wasn't the first time in his life he'd done it, but it was certainly the worst. This was the first time the mess he'd made of things was probably going to haunt him for the rest of his life.

He shouldn't have broken up with Molly. At least not like that—as if he'd just been pretending for the last two months, the way they'd intended. He should have told her the truth. He'd been afraid if he told her it wasn't fake but had to end anyway because he wanted children, she'd blame herself. Or maybe even feel pressured to change her mind.

He should have told her that he loved her, but that he was afraid he'd eventually feel unfulfilled and resentful if he gave up his dream of having a family. Maybe they would still have ended up in this spot, but at least she would know he loved her.

She deserved to know that. She should know that a man had loved her just the way she was, even if he'd broken both their hearts.

"Do you have any books about building beehives?"

Callan fixed a smile on his face and turned away from the framed black-and-white photo of the library he'd been staring blankly at. "I believe we do. Are you interested in keeping bees?"

"Absolutely not," the patron said as she followed him through the stacks. "But my husband is and he ordered some kind of starter kit from the internet, so now I have to learn everything about it so I can make sure he's doing it right."

Lucky him, Callan thought. "I'm sure the bees will appreciate that."

It didn't take long for him to find the woman a couple of books on the subject, and he also wrote down some helpful internet links he found while she browsed the new fiction titles. He'd taken a peek at her address and was relieved the bees would be residing on the other side of town.

Much to his dismay, Laura Thompson was the first patron to broach the subject. She came in to renew two books, which they both knew she could have done online. Lane's mother was such a nice lady and he'd hated lying to her about the dating. He was going to hate lying about the breakup even more.

"I hope the rumors about you and Molly breaking up aren't true," she told him, the sincerity in her eyes making his stomach hurt.

"They are, I'm afraid. It was mutual, though. We just want different things out of life." None of that was actually a lie. They'd mutually decided to break up the day they'd decided to fake date. And they did want different things from life.

"I'm sorry to hear that. You made such a lovely couple, and Paul and Amanda think the world of you."

The ache in his midsection spread to his chest. He thought the world of them, too. Sure, there were times he thought they could try a lot harder to understand their daughter, but they were nice people.

"Molly and I are still going to be friends, though I'm sure it'll be awkward for a little while."

"These things are always awkward for a while, especially in a tight community like ours. I hope you won't let it keep you away from the others, though. I know Lane likes you, and even though it won't be easy at first, you'll all move past this. You've become almost like family—and not just because you were dating our Molly—so give it time. And you're always welcome at the Thompson house, Callan."

Emotion welled up inside of him, clogging his

throat, so all he could do was nod for a moment until he got himself under control. "Thank you, Laura. That means a lot to me."

Once she'd gone and he was alone, Callan sat in his chair, put his elbows on his desk and buried his face in his hands, trying to process it all.

He wasn't alone anymore.

He'd come to Stonefield because he wanted to be a part of a community. He'd even gone along with an outlandish fake dating plan to protect his place in that community. And it had worked. He had a job he was thriving in. He was a part of a vibrant, tight-knit community. He had made good friends who, yes, were almost like a family to him. And he'd fallen in love with a warm, chaotic, funny woman who he now believed loved him, too.

Was that enough?

He didn't know. But there was one thing he *did* know for sure and that was the fact this life he'd built for himself in Stonefield was *not* enough without the woman he loved.

Molly sighed when a tear landed on the sticky note she'd just written, smudging some of the ink. It was still readable, though, and she wasn't sure if that was a good thing or bad.

1. Confirm any accommodations needed for service dog for Smith calling hours & service.

2. Return library books (because, UGH, of course they're due today).
3. Remind yourself over and over it was never real.

She knew she shouldn't have put number three on the list. Sure, it was technically actionable—a task she could check off at the end of the day. But it was going to hurt every time she looked at the sticky note, which would kick in her avoidance tendencies, and avoiding her number one tool for managing her life wasn't a good idea.

After crushing the sticky note in her hand, she tossed it across the room in the direction of the trash can. Of course she missed, but she'd pick it up later. She dried her eyes and took a few sips of her coffee. Then she took a fresh sticky note and started over.

1. Confirm accommodations for service dog for Smith calling hours & service.
2. Return library books.
3. Treat yourself to something decadent at the Perkin' Up Café because you're awesome and you're worth it.

That was much better. And if she hurried, she could drop the books in the book drop before the library even opened, and then go straight to number three. Once she was fully caffeinated and had shaken off the misery of a sleepless, tearful night, she'd lock herself in her office and tackle number one.

Unfortunately, fate in the form of her father had other plans. He and her mother had come across an accounting discrepancy with a supplier and it wasn't the first time. They'd both tried, but they couldn't nail down what was happening. Molly might not be the best at straight math, but she was excellent at finding patterns and solving puzzles, and they needed her to do it before the video sales conference Paul had with them that afternoon. He wasn't going to commit to more product if there was something shady going on.

It was almost lunchtime before she was able to tell her dad it looked like their software was charging several items incorrectly each time, but it seemed to be a glitch in the supplier's system and not deliberate on their part. Even though she wasn't in a great mood, she refrained from pointing out Amanda should have caught that a long time ago.

Of course she was too late to put her books in the book drop and run, since it was locked during their open hours. But she wasn't up to seeing Callan, so she renewed them online even though she'd already finished them and would probably drop them in the book drop in the morning.

Then again, if she held on to them for the two additional weeks, she should be past the initial hurt and be able to see Callan again without dying a little more inside. She wasn't giving up her library, so she was going to have to get over it at some point.

Just not today.

Hoping the lunch rush wouldn't start for a while, she went to the café to reward herself for her mad accounting puzzle skills with whatever caffeinated drink came with the most whipped cream.

"Oh honey," Chelsea said when she stepped up to the counter. "I don't even know what you're ordering, but I know it's going to need an extra shot of espresso. You look even worse than you did yesterday."

"I think yesterday it still didn't feel totally real. Today, it feels real. Also, I want extra whipped cream. Extra, extra whipped cream."

"You haven't actually ordered a drink to put it on yet," Chelsea pointed out.

"I want whatever comes with the most whipped cream."

Chelsea made her an iced macchiato with a huge swirl of whipped cream on top. And then she set the can next to the cup. "You get free whipped cream refills today."

The lunch rush was starting and Molly was in the way, so she took her drink and her whipped cream to her favorite table before somebody else got it. She was a quarter of the way through the macchiato and half the can of whipped cream when her phone chimed with a text message from Gwen.

Did you hear the library closed early today? I ran into Amy at the market and she said there's a sign on the door saying there was an emergency and regular hours will resume tomorrow.

Molly's pulse quickened at the thought of Callan having any kind of emergency, but she didn't give in to the immediate urge to call him or run out the door. He wasn't hers to worry about. He never had been, technically.

She typed a response to Gwen, though. Did you hear the librarian's none of my business anymore?

By watching the dots appear and disappear, she knew it took Gwen three tries to come up with a suitable response to that.

Okay.

Very Gwen, she thought. But then she thought maybe her own text message had been more rude than she'd intended and sent one more.

I'm sorry. Thank you for letting me know. Hopefully it's more of a plumbing emergency than a people emergency.

She got a thumbs-up emoji and a fingers crossed emoji in response, which Molly took to mean she was forgiven for being snarky and that Gwen hoped it was a plumbing emergency, too.

By the time she finished her macchiato—but not the whipped cream because apparently there was a limit to how much of a can a person could inhale—she couldn't take it anymore. Ruse or no ruse, they were still friends, weren't they? Or they would be eventually, when the sting wore off. That was what he said he wanted. Picking up her phone, she took a deep breath and pulled up the text message chain with Callan.

Are you okay? I heard there's a sign on the library door that says there's an emergency.

The response came so quickly, Callan must have had his phone in his hand.

Are you at home right now?

I'm at the café. What's going on?

Nothing bad. Can we meet at your place?

So much for her plan not to see Callan today. She couldn't imagine what the emergency could be, though, and she really wanted to know. It couldn't involve her family or any of Mallory's family because she would have heard before the librarian—probably. But she definitely would have heard by now. And she couldn't imagine what kind of library emergency she could help with.

But there was one way to find out.

I'll be there in a few minutes.

She didn't run because…well, she didn't run ever and if she tried, she'd probably only make it halfway before she'd have to call somebody to come pick her up. But she walked at a brisk enough pace so she was slightly out of breath when she turned the corner. Luckily, the pulse quickening that seeing Callan waiting outside her door caused wasn't enough to send her into cardiac arrest.

He inhaled sharply when he saw her and there was a nervous energy about him that Molly hadn't seen before. When she got close enough, he started to reach out, but then he shoved his hands in his pockets.

"Can we talk for a few minutes? Privately?"

"Of course." She led him up the stairs, wincing as she opened the door because she hadn't been at the top of her executive function game for the last couple of days and her apartment looked like a tropical storm "after" photo.

He didn't seem to notice. As soon as the door closed behind them, he ran one hand through his hair and blew out a breath. "I'm sorry, Molly. I shouldn't have ended things between us the way I did."

"I always knew it was coming. It's what I signed up for."

He shook his head. "No. What we had was absolutely not what we signed up for because it was real.

I didn't have the guts to tell you that, so I kept pretending it wasn't."

Hearing him finally say it took her breath away, and she owed him the same truth. "Yes, it was real. All of it."

"I know we agreed to fake date," he continued. "But what I felt—wanting to be near you and craving you and falling for you—none of that was ever fake. I never had to pretend you were the person I wanted to spend my time with."

Tears blurred her vision and she swiped them away with the back of her hand. "I never had to pretend I wanted to spend my time with you, either."

"Molly, I need you to know..." He stopped and breathed in slowly before taking something out of his pocket and holding it out to her.

It was a simple white folded card, like the kind you'd write a name on and set behind a plate for a dinner with assigned seating. And her name was written on the front in his tight, neat handwriting with one of the blue gel pens he favored.

Then she opened it and her breath caught in her chest.

I LOVE YOU!!!

He'd written the words in fat, red permanent marker with three exclamation points. And he'd underlined the word *LOVE* three times. There was even a lopsided heart doodle.

"All caps," he said, and though his voice sounded

rough, she couldn't take her eyes off the words on the card. "I'm not great at expressing myself in all caps, though I'm getting better at it with you in my life, but I wanted you to really *know* that I do love you in all caps."

"Callan," she whispered. "But—"

"I'd sit in the dark and drink questionable milk with you, Molly. I mean, we won't have to because I have my bills automatically paid online and I would buy fresh milk, but I would if that's where we ended up."

"I love you, too," she said, tears spilling onto her cheeks. "Not fake love, either. I really do love you."

She gave in to the impulse to throw herself into his arms and he caught her, holding her tight. His cheek pressed against the top of her head and they stayed that way for a long time. Molly closed her eyes and savored the feel of his arms around hers for the first *real* time.

"Laura came to see me at the library today," he said without letting her go. "She wanted me to know it would all be okay and they would all still be my friends and that I'm always welcome at her house."

"Laura's super nice."

"And when she said I was almost like family, it made me realize that I've been focused on having children to make a family for myself, but I'm becoming part of one. And you...*you* are my family."

She was shaking, a deep tremor that sometimes

happened when her emotions were becoming over-whelming. Pulling back slightly, she tipped her head to look up at him. "Speaking of our found family, Mallory helped me see that me not wanting a child because of the ADHD would be like if my parents had known and chosen not to have *me*. And it's hard sometimes, but I wouldn't give up my life. So maybe I shouldn't give up my hypothetical kids' lives."

She saw the understanding wash over him and the hope flare in his eyes. But he very gently set her away from him before cradling her cheek in his hand.

"I don't want you to make any choice because of me. It *is* your choice and I'm going to love you no matter what. I know that now and it's the truth."

"Do you know what Chelsea said to me? She asked me why my kid can't have a notebook."

"And sticky notes," he said.

"See?" She laughed and slapped his arm. "It made me think about how you took the time to research how my brain works. You let me talk through movies and you know how to distract me when I can't get out of my own head and all these ways that, instead of trying to make me be like you, you help being me be easier."

"I can color outside the lines with you," he promised. "And when there is coloring to be done that has to stay in the lines, then I'll hold the crayon."

"I believe you, because I've felt it. I know what it feels like to have your acceptance and support and I believe in my heart that when we have kids, they're going to thrive because you'll let them. I trust you to make them feel loved even when it's hard."

"When," he whispered. "You didn't say *if* we have kids. You said when."

"I think we'll have amazing kids, Callan. Amazing kids that will spend four hours watching one ant, but two minutes to brush their teeth is too much. And they'll remember every commercial jingle they've ever seen, but not where they left their retainers."

"Yes. And we'll advocate for them and love them and buy so many sticky notes we'll get Christmas cards from the office supply store." He brushed her hair back from her face. "I love you, Molly."

"I love you, too." Then she laughed because she couldn't contain her happiness anymore. "It feels so good to say that. I'm going to say it a lot, you know. Probably while you're trying to watch a movie."

"And I'll pause it even if it's a good part because there will never be anything I like more than hearing you say it."

"I'm a lot."

"Yes, you are. But you're never too much. You're just right for me."

Epilogue

Ten years later

"Roman Paul Avery, give your sister back her homework." Molly hated middle-naming her seven-year-old son, but he was on her last nerve today. He was like a mini version of her and rarely did a day pass when she didn't feel an urge to send her mother apology flowers. Or booze.

"I need it."

"Why do you need Hope's homework?"

He shrugged. "To help me with mine."

Hope, who was a year older than her brother and as neurotypical as her father, rolled her eyes. "You don't want help. You want to copy the answers, which is dumb because we're in different grades and our math is different, so they're not the same questions."

Molly dried her hands, thankful for a brief respite from washing the cabinet doors. They'd bought this big old house not far from the Sutton house two years ago and she loved it more than she'd thought it possible to love a house—except for the kitchen cabinets. They needed changing, but it wasn't easy to remodel a kitchen with two kids, so for now they stayed painted white and the paint wasn't new. They got dirty easily and she'd been putting off the task because she didn't want to do it.

"I'll help you," she told Rome—who was named after their dad's best friend who visited twice a year. "I'm not as good at math as your dad, but I'm sure we can figure out the answers together."

"It's not hard, Mom. I just don't want to do it. It's boring."

A feeling she knew well. The body doubling—having Hope doing her homework while he did his to keep him focused on what they were doing together—wasn't working and Callan wasn't home from work yet, so they'd do it Mom's way.

"If you get your math problems done and all correct before I finish washing the cupboard doors, you can have your tablet for fifteen extra minutes."

He was done before she'd refilled the sink with hot, soapy water. The right motivation worked wonders on that kid. Once she'd checked his work, he went to the chore chart and added a star sticker under *homework*. Making things a game and stickers almost always worked. Like mother, like son. If the kids would stop squabbling for a few minutes, she'd be able to add a star sticker to her list, too.

When the heard the front door open—thanks to the squeaky hinges she kept forgetting to oil—the kids ran to meet Callan in the foyer. She could hear their voices as they talked over each other to tell their dad everything about their day. It was usually at least two or three minutes before he was able to greet Molly, but his kisses were still worth the wait.

Having some free time between homework and dinner, Rome and Hope went upstairs, leaving Molly alone with her husband.

"How was the library today?" she asked after he'd kissed her thoroughly.

"Excellent. The plans came today. I brought them home to show you, but I left them in the car until the kids go to bed because if I don't, Rome will sneak down the stairs to color them in."

Molly laughed because he wasn't wrong. "I can't wait to see them."

Over the last decade, Callan had worked tirelessly to make the library into the heart of Stonefield, and it showed. They had a dedicated children's librarian now, along with several volunteer pages from the high school. And the town had finally approved the addition he'd been fighting for.

"And how was *your* day?" he asked, running his hands over her hips to pull her close.

"Messy. Very, very messy. Also, loud."

Not long after they'd gotten married, she'd gone

back to school and gotten the certifications she needed to be an elementary school art teacher. It didn't pay a lot, but the part-time hours were perfect, and she still helped her parents.

"Look what Hope painted today," she said, pointing to the newest picture on the front of the refrigerator.

It was a family portrait, and while their daughter was definitely not an art prodigy, it was easy to see that in the center was Callan with his stick arm around Molly, who had very unfortunate hair. To one side was Hope, who was wearing a long pink gown and a crown. And on the other side was Rome, who looked like he had mud on his face. She'd also included Tack, the neighbor's corgi, because she was on a mission to get a dog of her own.

"At least she got your hair right," Callan said, and Molly slapped his arm, laughing. "It's beautiful."

One of the things Molly loved most about her husband was how much he meant that. When she saw the warmth in his eyes as he looked at the crude painting, she knew he was seeing the only thing that mattered—their family.

"We're a lot," she said, tucking herself under his arm.

"Definitely a lot," he agreed, pressing a kiss to the top of her head. "But never too much."

* * * * *

#2959 FORTUNE'S DREAM HOUSE

The Fortunes of Texas: Hitting the Jackpot • by Nina Crespo

For Max Fortune Maloney to get his ranch bid accepted, he has to convince his agent, Eliza Henry, to pretend they're heading for the altar. Eliza needs the deal to advance her career, but she fears jeopardizing her reputation almost as much as she does falling for the sweet-talking cowboy.

#2960 SELLING SANDCASTLE

The McFaddens of Tinsley Cove • by Nancy Robards Thompson

Moving to North Carolina to be a part of a reality real estate show was never in newly divorced Cassie Houston's plans but she needs a fresh start. That fresh start was not going to include romance—still, the sparks flying between her and fellow costar Logan McFadden are impossible to deny. But they both have difficult pasts and sparks might not be enough.

#2961 THE COWBOY'S MISTAKEN IDENTITY

Dawson Family Ranch • by Melissa Senate

While looking for his father, rancher Chase Dawson finds an irate woman. *How could he abandon her and their son?* The problem is, Chase doesn't have a baby. But he does have a twin. Chase vows to right his brother's wrongs and be the man Hannah Calhoun and his nephew need. Can his love break through Hannah's guarded heart?

#2962 THE VALENTINE'S DO-OVER

by Michelle Lindo-Rice

When radio personalities Selena Cartwright and Trent Moon share why they've sworn off love and hate Valentine's Day, the gala celebrating singlehood is born! Planning the event has Trent and Selena seeing, and wanting, each other more than just professionally. As the gala approaches, can they overcome past heartache and possibly discover that Trent + Selena = True Love 4-Ever?

#2963 VALENTINES FOR THE RANCHER

Aspen Creek Bachelors • by Kathy Douglass

Jillian Adams expected Miles Montgomery to propose—she got a breakup speech instead! Now Jillian is back, and their ski resort hometown is heating up! Their kids become inseparable, making it impossible to avoid each other. So when the rancher asks Jillian for forgiveness and a Valentine's Day dance, can she trust him, and her heart, this time?

#2964 WHAT HAPPENS IN THE AIR

Love in the Valley • by Michele Dunaway

After Luke Thornton shattered her heart, Shelby Bien fled town to become a jet-setting photographer. Shelby's shocked to find that single dad Luke's back in New Charles. When they join forces to fly their families' hot-air balloon, it's Shelby's chance at a cover story. And, just maybe, a second chance for the former sweethearts' own story!

Get 4 FREE REWARDS!

We'll send you 2 FREE Books plus 2 FREE Mystery Gifts.

FREE Value Over **$20**

Both the **Harlequin® Special Edition** and **Harlequin® Heartwarming™** series feature compelling novels filled with stories of love and strength where the bonds of friendship, family and community unite.

YES! Please send me 2 FREE novels from the Harlequin Special Edition or Harlequin Heartwarming series and my 2 FREE gifts (gifts are worth about $10 retail). After receiving them, if I don't wish to receive any more books, I can return the shipping statement marked "cancel." If I don't cancel, I will receive 6 brand-new Harlequin Special Edition books every month and be billed just $5.49 each in the U.S. or $6.24 each in Canada, a savings of at least 12% off the cover price, or 4 brand-new Harlequin Heartwarming Larger-Print books every month and be billed just $6.24 each in the U.S. or $6.74 each in Canada, a savings of at least 19% off the cover price. It's quite a bargain! Shipping and handling is just 50¢ per book in the U.S. and $1.25 per book in Canada.* I understand that accepting the 2 free books and gifts places me under no obligation to buy anything. I can always return a shipment and cancel at any time by calling the number below. The free books and gifts are mine to keep no matter what I decide.

Choose one: ☐ **Harlequin Special Edition** (235/335 HDN GRJV) ☐ **Harlequin Heartwarming Larger-Print** (161/361 HDN GRJV)

Name (please print)

Address | Apt. #

City | State/Province | Zip/Postal Code

Email: Please check this box ☐ if you would like to receive newsletters and promotional emails from Harlequin Enterprises ULC and its affiliates. You can unsubscribe anytime.

Mail to the **Harlequin Reader Service:**
IN U.S.A.: P.O. Box 1341, Buffalo, NY 14240-8531
IN CANADA: P.O. Box 603, Fort Erie, Ontario L2A 5X3

Want to try 2 free books from another series! Call 1-800-873-8635 or visit www.ReaderService.com.

*Terms and prices subject to change without notice. Prices do not include sales taxes, which will be charged (if applicable) based on your state or country of residence. Canadian residents will be charged applicable taxes. Offer not valid in Quebec. This offer is limited to one order per household. Books received may not be as shown. Not valid for current subscribers to the Harlequin Special Edition or Harlequin Heartwarming series. All orders subject to approval. Credit or debit balances in a customer's account(s) may be offset by any other outstanding balance owed by or to the customer. Please allow 4 to 6 weeks for delivery. Offer available while quantities last.

Your Privacy—Your information is being collected by Harlequin Enterprises ULC, operating as Harlequin Reader Service. For a complete summary of the information we collect, how we use this information and to whom it is disclosed, please visit our privacy notice located at corporate.harlequin.com/privacy-notice. From time to time we may also exchange your personal information with reputable third parties. If you wish to opt out of this sharing of your personal information, please visit readerservice.com/consumerschoice or call 1-800-873-8635. **Notice to California Residents**—Under California law, you have specific rights to control and access your data. For more information on these rights and how to exercise them, visit corporate.harlequin.com/california-privacy.

HSEHW22R3

HARLEQUIN
PLUS

Try the best multimedia subscription service for romance readers like you!

Read, Watch and Play.

Experience the easiest way to get the romance content you crave.

Start your **FREE TRIAL** at
www.harlequinplus.com/freetrial.